one room Vacancy

AUTHOR'S NOTE

One Room Vacancy is a story of longing, closure, and learning how to stay when it matters most. While the story unfolds in a familiar setting with characters you've met before, it explores more emotionally vulnerable terrain and touches on aspects of the human experience that may be difficult for some.

ORV includes depictions and mentions of the death of a parent (past-tense, off page), emotional abuse, alcoholism, manipulation, and mental health struggles—all of which take place outside the central relationship—and includes sexually explicit content. This is intended for adult audiences.

Please know that these topics were approached with the utmost care and dedication to accuracy and proper representation.

For Arianna,
Now shut the hell up about it.

*For the ones who still replay the what-ifs.
The ones who wish he'd woken up and chosen you—but know deep
down he never would've. This isn't your happy ending, but maybe it
helps you let go of his.*

PLAYLIST

F&MU by Kehlani
Call Me When You Break Up by Selena Gomez, Benny Blanco, and Gracie
Abrams
Truth Hurts by Lizzo
Manchild by Sabrina Carpenter
Nunya by Kehlani & Dom Kennedy
The Tortured Poets Department by Taylor Swift
Us by Gracie Abrams & Taylor Swift
Already Over by Sabrina Carpenter
Obsessed by Olivia Rodrigo
Please Please Please by Sabrina Carpenter
Style by Taylor Swift
Crazy for This Girl by Evan And Jaron
The Alchemy by Taylor Swift
Something, Somehow, Someday by Role Model

PROLOGUE
SAGE

First and foremost, I'd like to reinforce that I am not bitching that I'm single. I'm elated that I'm not in a relationship roughly ninety-five percent of the time, and today is no different. Except for when Liam left right after Hannah, Gen left with Jackson, Gabe left with Kara, Wes left with Savannah, and I left for the hotel with my rosebud in the front pocket of my duffel bag. I'll admit...I was feeling a little jaded.

For a hotel this nice, you'd think they would have taken the time to scrape the old popcorn texture off the ceiling. But as I notice I've been lying here, staring up at the oddly unsettling texture for over half an hour, I realize just how pathetic I'm being.

I'm single by choice, damn it. I enjoy answering to no one but myself. That, and no guy has ever really held my attention for more than a night or two. Well, one, but that's beside the point.

When everyone paired off to leave for the hotel where Jackson and Gen's wedding would be held tomorrow, I knew a night full of jack shit was in store for me. Apparently, once paired up, you become a stick in the mud who can't be bothered to take a detour to the hotel bar for a couple of hours before going to bed at the nice geriatric time of 10:30 PM.

When did my friends become so boring?

My phone dings on the bedside table, a welcome reprieve from my methodical counting of the plastered bumps taunting me from above. I lay my head back against the pillow as I open my text messages.

GABE

still wanna grab that drink?

Gabe and I don't hang out alone often. Actually, I'm pretty sure the last time we were alone together was the last time he and Kara broke up. Well, maybe not *last*—two times ago, maybe?

It's never been a secret that I'm attracted to him, but I'm no homewrecker. Then again, it's hard to wreck a home that's been stripped down to studs from years of fighting and breaking up every other week.

It doesn't matter, though. Shitty human or not, Kara is Gabe's girlfriend. An on-and-off girlfriend he's horrible with and no one supports, but a girlfriend nonetheless.

SAGE

you and kara?

nah, just me.

That's...ominous.

she get tired of walking on stilts to reach your shoulders?

something like that.

Gnawing at my inner cheek, I find myself questioning if going down to the hotel bar is a horrible idea. I'm sure they broke up again. If he needed comfort, he'd text Liam. But I suppose there are a multitude of ways someone may seek comfort; I'm just not sure, with his and Kara's track record of getting back together, if entertaining that idea is wise...for either of us.

did she leave?

yeah, i'm almost to the hotel, i dropped her at home before leaving the city.

??

I don't miss the way he ignores my questioning. He seldom wants to talk about what drives them to break up. Liam has shared bits and pieces about their relationship over the years, and none of it has been good. How can Gabe stay with someone his best friend hates so passionately—for *years*?

so, drinks?

This could quite possibly be the worst idea I've ever had, and I very well might hate myself tomorrow, but at this moment, I can't will myself to care.

yeah, drinks.

I shoot up from where I was lying and glance around the room, debating whether to change out of the dress I wore to the rehearsal dinner. Leggings sound like the obvious move, but let's be real—I look hot. Booty call or not, it feels criminal to waste this dress after only a few hours of glory.

I step in front of the mirror and catch the way the deep orange satin glows against my medium brown skin. *Damn.* I groan, half in appreciation, half in resignation, and make my way to the dresser. I grab a hairpin from my makeup bag and attempt to rescue what's left of the updo I so painstakingly perfected earlier. Lying down definitely didn't help.

Maybe it's time for a hair change again. The caramel highlights are cute, but I've never kept one color this long since I started dyeing it at eighteen. Maybe I'll go back to dark brown. Or—screw it—maybe it's finally time for purple.

I slip into my gold heels, one foot at a time, and give myself a final once-over before stepping into the hall. My stomach flips with every click of my heels against the marble floor on the way to the hotel bar.

It's not that I don't like being around Gabe. I do. Probably too much. But being the girl he calls every time Kara kicks him to the curb? That's started to feel a little cheap. And given the situation, the last thing I want is to admit to any of our friends that we've hooked up more than once. It's messy. It's complicated. And I'd look pathetic.

So, I do what any average woman in her twenties would do...I do it anyway, and I don't tell anyone about it.

My heels clack against the marble flooring of the hotel bar as I approach, my eyes falling to the all-too-familiar man sitting at the end, leaning against the lacquered bar top.

Even leaning against the bar, he towers at least a head above the rest of the guys in the room. That's part of what drew me in the first time I saw him—out on the golf course, standing next to my brother and their friends, larger than life with that wild red hair and a smile that could melt the panties off a nun.

But I learned pretty quickly that there was a major problem.

"You and Kara break up again?" I ask as I approach, trying—and mostly failing—to slide into the cool, detached version of myself I like to present around men. Well, most men. Gabe's always managed to bulldoze right through it.

He exhales hard, scratching the back of his neck. Classic Gabe.

That move always means he's uncomfortable. "Yeah. It just wasn't working anymore. Hasn't been for a while."

"No shit," I mutter, my tone sharper than I meant it to be. I expect him to brush it off like usual, throw me one of his easy smiles or fire back with something sarcastic.

But he doesn't.

Instead, he looks at me—and there's something raw behind his gaze. The exhaustion. The defeat. It catches me off guard, this version of him. The one without the armor. Unfortunately, that is my least favorite form of Gabe.

"Are you okay?" My voice softens.

He pauses for a moment before nodding. "Yeah, I'm fine. It had to happen."

That should be what I want to hear, that they're really done, but I've been here before. "Are you two done for good?"

Gabe says nothing, just nods. It hardly instills confidence, yet I take his response at face value because it's what I want to hear.

Pathetic, I know.

"And you're sure you're okay?" I ask, genuinely concerned by the answer. This isn't the first time I've seen him this defeated, and I hate it. He doesn't deserve this; he never has. I don't understand the hold she has on him, but it can't be good for him.

"Yeah, I'm fine." He sighs as he lifts a pint glass to his lips and downs half his beer in three slow gulps.

Fine, I'm sure.

"Do you want to talk about it?"

He shakes his head. I swivel back and forth on my heels, trying to think of how to proceed, but everything I can think of would just cause me to sound pathetic. So, I put up my typical facade.

"Well, as fun as this has been, you seem content by yourself, so I'm going to go..."

With no hesitation, Gabe reaches out and delicately takes hold of my wrist with one hand. His touch is both gentle and strong, easily keeping me from moving. His hand, with its fair complexion and roughness from hard work, encircles my wrist effortlessly.

"Please don't go," he whispers, so softly that I almost miss it, but the sincerity in his plea causes me to abandon my plan of leaving the bar.

Our gazes lock and I swallow hard, seeing the man I've come to care for over the years looking back at me with a brokenness that exceeds his towering frame. "All right."

An hour and a half passes, along with four glasses of Bordeaux, and I'm feeling a bit tipsy. Gabe, on the other hand, is still sulking.

I playfully nudge his cheek with my finger, prompting a small, dimpled smile to form on his lips. "C'mon. Buck up, Buttercup!" I say in an effort to cheer him up.

His attempts at hiding his grin are futile as he laughs. "I hate when you call me that."

"It's a common phrase."

"It's corny."

"It's the south; it's supposed to be a little corny."

The bartender places the checks in front of us, silently indicating that they closed twenty minutes ago. It is a not-so-subtle hint for us to finish up and leave, and without missing a beat, Gabe grabs both receipts and sets his card on top of them.

Once the bartender retrieves his card, Gabe shifts in his seat and positions his body to face me, his hand resting on my knee. "Thank you for coming down tonight. It means a lot."

"Of course. Who better to distract you, right?"

He pauses, unmoving, as his gaze locks on mine, a serious expression plaguing his brow. "It's not like that."

A lump forms in my throat. "Then what is it like?"

"I like spending time with you, distraction or not."

"Then why do you only call or text when you and Kara break up?"

As soon as I ask, I see it—tension rolling through his shoulders, tightening his posture beneath the crisp fabric of his shirt. The bartender returns with his card, receipt, and pen, and he doesn't say a word until she walks away. Then he exhales, slow and heavy, like the weight of the moment just caught up with him.

He signs the merchant copy, and I don't miss the slight tremble in his hand.

"I'm sorry I've been doing that," he says quietly. "I never meant to. It's just—" His voice fades, eyes fixed on the bar like he's somewhere else entirely. Somewhere he doesn't want to be.

"Kara didn't trust me."

Gabe hesitates with the pen hovering over the scrap of receipt paper. "It was never about trusting you."

My brows nearly hit my hairline at his implication. "So she just didn't trust you...with me?"

He nods.

"Why?" I ask, knowing why but wanting him to say it. This song and dance we do, this falling together whenever he's sure they're over... It's exhausting, but more than anything I want him to acknowledge it. I'm not crazy—I know there is something here, so why does it always get avoided when I want him to verbalize it?

"She...could tell, I guess?" His shoulders hunch forward as he scrunches them in frustration.

"Tell what?"

He doesn't mince his words, doesn't resist the urge to blurt them out; rather, he speaks matter-of-factly. "That I'm into you."

"You are?!" I gasp, feigning shock at his admission.

He grins and teasingly pinches my side before standing up and leading us toward the exit of the bar and into the hotel lobby.

And that's when the unspoken question hangs heavy in the space between us. He doesn't say it—doesn't have to. With our history, it's always there, humming beneath the surface. But the way he shifts on the balls of his feet, like he's already halfway gone, tells me everything I need to know.

He's not going to ask me to come with him.

Maybe this is who we've always been meant to be. Friends. Confidants. Orbiting each other with just enough gravity to stay close, but never enough to collide. And yet, he's still the only person I've ever wanted *more* with.

"I should get to bed," he says finally. "Haven't even really been up to my room yet. Just dropped my bag and came down here."

He steps in without waiting for permission, tilts his head down, and presses a soft kiss to my crown. It's gentle. Final. A silent promise to stay right where we are.

Then he steps back with a sigh and that familiar, bittersweet smile.

"Good night, Sage."

"Good night, Gabe." I try to hide my disappointment, but it's obvious in my voice. Despite this, I swivel on my heel and begin to walk in the opposite direction toward the elevator.

"Hey, Sage?" The man who is typically eerily confident with me sounds far more defeated than I've ever heard him, making me think that maybe, just maybe, he and Kara are really over this time.

"Hm?" I ask, turning my head to face him.

"I'm sorry...for always doing this. I promise we're over, if that means anything. It's been over for a long time; I just refused to face it."

"It's okay. I'm not going to be the person to start claiming I have the healthiest of coping mechanisms either. Gotta handle it how you handle it, ya know?"

He nods in understanding before turning back around to walk away.

"Wait." My voice echoes through the lobby, and I'm surprised at how quickly it leaves my lips. I know this isn't a good idea. I've been in this situation too many times before, despite his assurance that things are over between him and Kara. But when his gaze meets mine with a puzzled look on his face, I can't help but smile. I motion toward the elevator, silently urging him to join me.

"Are you sure?" he asks.

I nod with a smile. "I'm sure."

ONE

GABE

My fingertips trail slowly up the inside of her thigh, tracing the soft curve of her leg. She sucks in a quiet breath, and the sound alone sends heat rushing through me. It's been too long since I've touched her—too long since this thing between us felt real enough to hold onto.

We're tangled on the couch in her hotel room, which happens to be a mirror image of mine down the hall. Her legs are draped across mine, bare skin flush against satin, and the late summer heat clings to us in the air between kisses. She smells like her favorite perfume and just a hint of sweat, and fuck if that isn't the most dangerous combination in the world.

Every time she gasps, every time her lips part for me, I want to memorize the sound. Because this? This might be one of the rare times I get to pretend she's mine.

She leans in just enough to make my pulse skip, and I meet her halfway, catching her mouth in a kiss that tastes like want and regret, all wrapped into one. It burns through me, hungry and reckless.

We shouldn't be doing this.

We never should be doing this.

But it's Sage—and that's all it ever takes to make me forget tomorrow exists.

This woman.

She's chaos and gravity, and I've never figured out how to escape her pull. Since the day I met her on that stupid golf course two years ago, she's been under my skin, in my head, haunting every quiet moment. I've spent years trying not to want her—failing every single time.

I need her. God, I need her.

But I don't get to keep her—not really. Not for long. With every ounce of determination, I pry my lips away from hers and trail a line of kisses down her neck. The intoxicating flavor of her skin sets me aflame, igniting an all-consuming frenzy within me. Every touch, every taste, sends shivers down my spine as I eagerly explore every inch of her exposed skin.

"Gabe," Sage gasps, pulling my attention to her kiss-swollen lips, her smudged lipstick from this evening a stark contrast to the otherwise poised woman I know. She doesn't need to tell me what she needs, but that doesn't make the words any less sweet as they roll off her tongue. "Touch me."

With a hunger that matches the intensity in Sage's eyes, I lean in closer, my breath mingling with hers. I can feel her heart racing against my chest, and I revel in it. Without a word, I trace my fingertips further up her thigh as my lips graze down her neck, feeling the electricity of her skin with every touch.

Sage lets out a soft sigh, closing her eyes as she surrenders to the sensation. My fingers dance over the hem of her panties, leaving a trail of fire in their wake.

I need her, and only a tiny slip of fabric separates me from exactly what I crave.

As I slowly slide my finger under the lace of her panties, I can feel the warmth of her skin against my fingertips, and I shiver at the anticipation. Sage's eyes flutter open, and she looks at me with a mixture of fear and excitement that only adds to the intensity between us.

"Are you sure about this?" I ask, wanting to make sure we're both on the same page. We've been here before, and it didn't end well. But the desire in her eyes speaks louder than any words could ever say. She nods, her lips parted slightly as she watches my every move.

I breathe her in through the fabric, touch her for the first time in what feels like forever. It's like flipping a switch—suddenly, every nerve in my body is alive, burning up with the way she arches into my hand, gasping just under her breath.

"Gabe," she whispers.

And just as I slide that teasing strip of lace to the side—

Ice. Cold. Water.

It hits me square in the face, sharp and shocking, running down my neck like a slap. I jolt upright with a gasp, sputtering and shaking, heart racing for a very different reason now.

My eyes snap open—and instead of Sage's face, I get a full view of Liam. Grinning like the smug bastard he is, holding an empty glass and absolutely no remorse.

"Dude, what the fuck?" I groan, dragging a hand down my soaked face.

My hair's dripping, clinging to my forehead, and when I shove the glass away, the rest of the water spills straight onto his brand-new sneakers.

"Shit," he yelps, hopping backward as he rights the cup. He looks annoyed for about two seconds—then he sees my glare and just laughs. "You sleep like the dead when you drink. I was starting to worry."

"So, naturally, your solution was waterboarding."

"Please. That was six ounces, max." He swats my leg until I move it, trying to drop down onto the couch like this is totally normal—but only manages to half-settle, awkwardly balancing when I don't budge.

He should have thought about that before trying to drown me in my sleep.

Taking my stubbornness in stride, he sits down on my calves without a care in the world while shoving a piece of toast into his mouth.

Liam and I have been inseparable since we were teenagers, our friendship standing the test of time. His playful nature and occasional immaturity only added to his charm, making him the best friend anyone could ask for. He never judged me, even though he had no qualms about judging others for their actions.

But there was one thing Liam couldn't understand or accept: my relationship with my ex, Kara. It seemed like everyone else in our circle judged me for it, too, but while Liam didn't hide his disdain for our relationship, he respects me enough to have allowed me to let things pan out the way I needed them to.

Liam's phone dings, causing him to shift on my legs and tweak my knee a little.

"Move," I sternly groan, and he lifts onto his feet, his cell phone clutched tightly in his hands as his fingers move at the speed of light. "Hannah?" I ask.

He looks up at me, almost like a puppy caught getting into a hamper filled with dirty laundry, and just shrugs before saying, "Yeah."

If there is one relationship that makes less sense to me than my past with Kara, it is Liam and Hannah. Despite having been at each other's throats for as long as I've known them, they managed to fall in love in the most unlikely of circumstances. He's in the doghouse right now while Hannah is on tour, but I have a feeling, with how much they've been talking, that their story isn't over.

"How's that going?" I ask, nodding toward his phone. He's been a little more open about it since we saw her in Chicago, but he still gets cagey sometimes. I think it has to do with her family, though I don't fully get it—he's known them forever. Then again, I get messy family dynamics more than most.

"Good," he says, short and clipped, sliding his phone into his pocket and rocking on his heels. "You ready for today?"

If getting blackout drunk last night counts as being ready, then sure. "Yeah, man. I'm ready."

We're heading to the apartment Kara and I used to share—my final box retrieval mission. I've been dodging it since the breakup. But now, with no more excuses, no more delays, it's like everything's crashing in at once. This is the longest we've ever gone without talking since we met. Maybe that's a good thing. Maybe it means we're finally done. Still, something about it doesn't sit right.

"She won't be there?" Liam asks, voice edged with curiosity.

"Nope. Works Saturdays. Starts at eleven." I shrug, trying to play it cool.

He doesn't say anything, just grabs the key from the bowl by the door. It's got one of those obnoxiously bright orange U-Haul tags on it. Like a warning sign. Or maybe a clean slate.

Either way, this is really happening. And I won't know how I feel about it until it's done.

We're halfway down the sidewalk when Liam turns to me. "You ever talk to Wes?"

TWO

SAGE

The Harry's bag hits the entryway table with a dull thud as I kick off my sneakers and let out a dramatic, soul-deep sigh. Tuesdays are usually dead, borderline comatose, but today was pure chaos. And as the only bartender on from open to close, I'm about one toe cramp away from sawing my feet off, *Saw I*-style, and calling it a night.

A loud knock jars the stillness. Sharp. Repetitive.

I flinch.

For a second, I consider pretending I'm not home, but whoever it is isn't giving up. With a groan, I shuffle to the door and crack it open.

Wes.

"Why are yo—" I start, but he breezes past me like he owns the place.

Which, technically, he does.

"By all means," I call after him, "make yourself at home."

He grins, shaking his head. "I own your apartment."

"Landlords aren't supposed to just barge in."

"You don't pay rent."

"Semantics." I wave him off. "Why even knock, then? Why not use your precious key?"

"Because last time I did that," he says dryly, "you had a guy over. In the kitchen."

A laugh bursts out of me—loud and unfiltered. The memory flashes through my mind: Wes walking in, face pale, eyes wide, immediately retreating like the kitchen was on fire. It wasn't even me he got an eyeful of, which made it that much funnier, and thankfully probably a bit less traumatizing.

"That's what you get for not knocking," I tease, smirking.

"Exactly why I did knock this time."

"Fair enough," I say, padding into the kitchen. I grab a cold Sweetwater 420 from the fridge and hold it up. He nods, already settling in like he lives here.

Two cans in hand, I head back to the living room and hand him one without a word.

"So what's up?" I ask as I pop the tab on my beer. It's unlike him to show up unannounced, especially not after eight o'clock at night. My brother's blue scrubs are rumpled and splattered with what I hope are just food stains after a long shift at the hospital, so I can't imagine what's so important.

"Do I need a reason to stop by and see my only sister?" He raises a brow.

"Oh, bullshit." I laugh awkwardly. "What's going on?"

Wes rubs the back of his neck in that way he does when Dad is pissing him off or Savannah tells him she bought another unplanned handbag because her Hermes sales associate called her with something she "couldn't resist."

"Wes…" My voice pitches lower. "What's going on?"

"You're getting a new roommate."

"Oh…well." I bite my inner cheek, trying to think of a way to sway his decision. "I don't want a roommate."

"Well, you're getting one."

"I refuse to live with another stranger."

"Wouldn't be a stranger."

I stare at him for a few seconds, trying to think of who it could possibly be.

"So, Gabe and Kara broke up."

"And the sky is blue."

"They lived together…"

"And? They'll be back together next week."

"They're not getting back together."

I scoff.

"I'm serious—they're done."

"Whether I believe you or not, I don't want him living here."

"He doesn't have anywhere to go."

"Then get an Airbnb."

"He's moving in, Sage."

I groan as my brother exits my apartment—his apartment, technically.

It isn't that I dislike Gabe; I just don't want to share a residence with him. It's too complicated. However, I can't tell Wes that. As far as he knows, I just have a petty dislike for the man.

After Wes leaves, I pace the living room for a while, beer in hand, flipping through a dozen rebuttals I should've made to change his mind. But none of them matter. He's already made the call. Gabe Keaton is moving in.

I don't want him here. I don't want him anywhere near my space or my peace or my half-stocked fridge. But, more than anything, I don't want the version of me I used to be around him. The one who made excuses, the one who let a handful of moments rewrite years of messy silence.

Eventually, when my phone buzzes with a "you still coming?" text from Savannah, I grab my keys and head out.

Later that night, Savannah sets a glass of red wine down in front of me with an awkward look on her face. She pulls out a different bottle of white from the fridge and pours her own glass. I've been staring into the abyss of her marble countertop for ten full minutes, replaying the earlier conversation with Wes on a loop.

"So, are you going to tell him Gabe can't move in?" I ask for the second time since getting here twenty minutes ago.

"You know I don't have that kind of power...and I'm not sure I'd want to, anyway." She lets out a sigh before collapsing onto the barstool next to me. "Besides, I thought you'd be excited. You've always had a crush on him."

Yeah yeah, the never-ending reminder from everyone in our friend group. I should find it embarrassing, but more than anything, it just pisses me off.

From the moment I laid eyes on Gabe, I was captivated. His charm and confidence drew me in. But as time went on, the infatuation cracked. He's manipulative, self-serving, toxic...not the guy I thought he was.

There's one memory I haven't been able to shake. After Gen's birthday party, we were the last two to leave. He walked me to my car, lingered a little too long by the door. Said I looked pretty when I wasn't trying—and then disappeared for three weeks. No text. No call. Just ghosted, like the words meant nothing. Like I meant nothing.

"Not anymore," I say.

Savannah takes a sip from her glass, her face contorting as she sets it down, fingers fidgeting. "I haven't even told your brother yet, but I just found out I'm pregnant and I don't know what to do."

My mind races. This is unexpected and, honestly, makes my roommate crisis feel small. "What exactly are you freaking out about?"

Her eyes meet mine, wide with uncertainty. "I don't know if I'm ready for this. I've never been a mother before."

"You're going to be a great mom...and Wes is going to be a great dad. Did I ever tell you he used to steal my baby dolls?"

Savannah chuckles. "You've never told me that."

"Well, he would usually draw on them before being forced to give them back, but chances are he would never do that to your baby."

"How reassuring."

"Have you been to a doctor?"

She nods. "Last week. I'm seven weeks along."

"When are you planning to tell Wes?"

"Soon."

I reach over and place a hand on hers. "You're going to be an amazing mother."

"You don't know that."

"I do. Because you're one of the most loving people I know. A bit overreaching at times...and definitely invasive..."

"Get to your point, please."

"You care. This baby would be no different."

Savannah softens. "Thanks, Sage."

"It's what I'm here for. What if not to reassure you and drive my brother insane simultaneously?"

She laughs, hand resting instinctively on her still-flat stomach.

"Which—speaking of my brother—what the hell was he thinking with this Gabe shit?"

Savannah shrugs. "Can't say for sure, but it won't be as bad as you think."

"You don't know that."

"Well...you could avoid fucking him, for one."

"You said you wouldn't bring that up again."

"I said I wouldn't *randomly* bring that up again. But it is very relevant here."

"Well, I don't plan to. I fully intend to avoid him like the plague."

"That apartment isn't exactly big, Sage."

"Don't care. I'm going to set some ground rules and try to make this as pain-free as possible."

"By not fucking him?"

"Suck my dick, Sav," I laugh.

"Love you too!"

THREE

FOUR MONTHS AGO

SAGE

The elevator ride is quiet.

Not awkward, not tense—just quiet. The kind of silence that hums in your gut like a warning, like you already know this is a bad idea and your body is waiting for your brain to catch up.

I don't look at him, but I can feel him. That's the thing with Gabe—he doesn't just take up space; he owns it. Heat radiates off him like static, this quiet pull that's always been there, just beneath the surface, even when we pretend it's not.

My hands are folded in front of me, fingers knotted too tight, like they're trying to hold the rest of me together. Gabe shifts beside me. I hear the soft crack of his knuckles and the faint sigh that follows. He's nervous, and that almost makes it worse—because I know how careful he is when it comes to me. Like he's afraid to break something we never even admitted we had.

The elevator dings.

I lead the way to my room, every step padded and slow. I don't trust myself to speak, so I don't. I just open the door, step inside, and wait for him to follow.

He does.

The door clicks shut behind us.

For a second, we just stand there. I kick off my heels, my toes sinking into the plush carpet. Gabe's hands hang at his sides, fingers flexing and unflexing like he's still deciding. Whether to speak, whether to stay, whether this is what he wants or what he's just used to.

I should stop this. I know that.

Instead, I take a step toward him.

His eyes lock on mine like a magnet finding its pull. "Sage," he says, and it's not a question, not a warning—just my name, heavy with whatever this is between us.

"I know," I whisper.

But I don't touch him. Not yet.

The space between us is thin, but it hums just the same. That taut, electric kind of pressure that doesn't need to be loud to feel dangerous. My pulse stutters at the base of my throat. Gabe shifts, barely—just enough that the fabric of his button-down rustles in the quiet. I catch a glimpse of the muscle in his jaw as it tightens, like he's holding something back.

Not guilt.

Something heavier. Something careful.

"I don't want to make this worse," he says, voice low. "For you."

I let out a dry little laugh, more scoff than sound. "What, you think this is me spiraling?"

He doesn't answer right away. His jaw clenches. "No. I think this is us...circling."

He's not wrong, but I don't say that.

Instead, I lift my chin. "You're not that powerful, Gabe. You're not capable of breaking me."

His gaze flickers—hurt, maybe, or admiration, I can't tell.

"I don't want to," he says.

"Then don't."

Another beat of silence. I step closer, close enough to count his freckles. Close enough that if he breathes too hard, we'll touch.

His fingers twitch again. Still flexing, still not reaching.

"Say it," I murmur. "Whatever's rattling around in that ginger head of yours."

He looks at me like he's torn between kissing me and bolting.

Then, finally—finally—he says, "I want you."

That's all I need.

I move first.

Just a breath closer, my hand lifting on instinct, fingertips grazing the front of his shirt, brushing the line of buttons like I'm not sure whether I'm smoothing fabric or testing the strength of whatever's still holding me back.

He doesn't flinch, doesn't step away.

But he doesn't reach for me either.

His breath stirs the curls by my temple. "Sage," he says again— same tone, same weight, but this time it's strained, like he's fighting the part of him that wants to ruin this distance completely.

I look up at him, and I mean *look*, really look, because I need him to see it in my eyes before either of us does something we can't take back.

"I'm not drunk," I say. "Just so we're clear."

"Neither am I."

"Good."

"Good."

"Great."

"Fantastic." The word slips past his lips as his eyes linger on my own. He's still holding back.

My fingers slide upward, finding the edge of his collar, tracing along the base of his neck where the skin is warm, flushed. "Because if we're going to do this again, I want it honest."

His jaw ticks. "We?"

I raise a brow. "You said you wanted me."

"I do."

"Then stop waiting for permission."

That's all it takes.

He surges forward like he's letting go of the last shred of restraint he's been holding onto. One hand lands at my waist, the other sliding up to cradle the back of my neck as his mouth finds mine—hungry, careful, like he's trying to memorize it before I can change my mind. I don't. I won't.

I kiss him back just as hard.

And when he pulls me flush against his chest, when his hand fists in the back of my dress and my fingers tangle in his hair, all the hesitation disappears.

This isn't a mistake.

This is combustion.

His mouth parts mine on a groan, the sound low and guttural like it's been building in his chest for years. Maybe it has. His tongue brushes mine and my knees nearly give, but he's there—one arm banded around my waist, holding me up like he's not letting me go this time.

I clutch his shirt, the fabric stretching between us until I finally yank it free from where it's tucked into his pants. My hands slide beneath, fingertips grazing bare skin and the hard plane of his stomach. He shudders.

"Fuck," he mutters against my mouth, pulling back just enough to look at me. His eyes search mine, pupils blown, breath uneven. "Tell me to stop."

"I won't."

That's all it takes. His mouth is on mine again, rougher this time, less careful. He walks me backward toward the bed without breaking the kiss, and when my legs hit the edge of the mattress, he pauses only to yank off his shirt.

I've seen him shirtless before—more times than I'll ever admit out loud—but never like this.

Not with that look in his eyes.

Not with this kind of finality.

Because if he and Kara are really done, then we don't get to pretend anymore.

Then this isn't just a quick fuck when we're both marginally single—it's a reckoning.

And if he could actually stay...

I have to admit I might want him to.

He kisses me like he hears that thought—like it's loud and gasping and written all over my skin.

The backs of my knees hit the mattress, and I sink into it, bracing on my elbows, staring up at him as he sheds the last of his restraint. His eyes rove down my body, slow and reverent, like he's trying to burn the image into memory. Like he already knows this won't be enough, but he's going to take it anyway.

"Come here," I breathe.

He does.

One knee presses into the mattress, then the other, and he crawls toward me like he's trying not to spook whatever this is between us.

His hands skim up my calves, slow and steady, pushing the hem of my dress higher as he goes.

"Been thinking about this all night," he mutters, eyes fixed on the sliver of bare skin he's uncovering. "This fuckin' dress—"

He bends down, mouth brushing my knee, then higher, then again.

"Didn't even hear half of what Jackson was saying at dinner. Just kept looking at you...lookin' like that."

I huff out a breath. "Like what?"

His mouth drags up the inside of my thigh. "Like trouble."

I arch a brow. "You've had me before, Gabe. You know what I'm like."

He shakes his head, kisses the dip between my hip and thigh. "Not like this."

His voice is muffled against my skin, like he's not even talking to me anymore—just saying it because it's the only way to let it out.

"That color on you—shit, I don't even usually have an opinion on dresses, but I wanted to lose my mind."

My breath catches. His hands are on my waist now, palms warm and wide, sliding the fabric up and over my hips, slow, like he's unwrapping something fragile. He leans in again, presses a kiss to the soft skin just below my belly button.

"I couldn't stop thinkin' about the idea of gettin' my hands on you." Another kiss. "Mouth on you." His voice dips lower. "You all spread out like this."

"Gabe." My voice cracks a little.

He glances up, hair falling into his eyes. "Just tell me to stop."

"I won't."

He sinks lower between my thighs, dragging his mouth along my skin like he's starved for it. No more talking, just heat.

He hooks his fingers in the sides of my underwear that is barely a sliver of fabric, eyes flicking up one last time to check, really check, but I don't look away. I lift my hips for him.

They're gone in a second, tossed somewhere neither of us cares about.

He groans under his breath, a sound like he's physically trying to keep it together, and presses a kiss to the inside of my thigh. Then another, higher.

And then he licks a long, slow stripe up the center of me, and my whole body jerks.

"Fuck," he mutters, barely audible. "Missed this."

I squeeze my eyes shut.

Not because of what he's doing—because God, that feels incredible—but because I know he means it. I know he means this.

The sex, the way I taste, the way I sound when he's got his mouth on me like this. That's what he misses.

Not me.

Not my laugh or the way I make him coffee after a night he snuck over to my place, even when I'm pissed at him. Not how I remember which songs he skips on an album in the car or that he cracks his knuckles when he's thinking.

Just this.

And maybe that should be enough, maybe it has to be.

Because if he and Kara are really done, if this isn't just a one-time thing to blow off steam...then we'd have to talk about what it means.

We'd have to stop pretending.

And I don't think either of us is ready for that.

So, I arch toward him instead. I bury my hand in his hair and let myself fall back against the pillows, breath caught in my throat.

He doesn't ease into it. Doesn't tease.

He just settles in like it's instinct. Like he knows exactly how to touch me, because he does—he always has.

His tongue works in lazy, confident strokes at first—measured, almost like he's savoring every second. But when my hips lift toward him and I thread my fingers through his hair with a breathless gasp, he groans into me and shifts closer. His hands grip my thighs, pulling me to the edge, anchoring me there.

One hand slides up, thumb finding that perfect pressure point, and I break.

I gasp, thighs tensing around his shoulders.

He groans again, this time louder. "God, Sage..." It's wrecked, worshipful. "You're so fuckin' sweet."

I laugh—more of a choked, breathless sound, because it's the least suave thing he could've said.

But he means it; that's the worst part.

I can feel it in the way his mouth moves, the way he shifts to get deeper, to keep going, to give.

I clutch at the sheets with one hand, his hair with the other, and let go of every reason this shouldn't be happening.

Because it is.

And, for one stupid second, it almost feels like more.

Like maybe he means it the way I do, or...sometimes do. In moments of weakness.

But that's not what this is—that's never what this is.

I force the thought out of my head like it burned me. Dig my fingers into his copper strands a little harder, not to guide him, just to ground myself.

Because the second I start pretending this is anything but sex, I lose.

Gabe doesn't get to be more. Not again.

He gets to be this—hot mouth, rough hands, the sound he makes when I fall apart for him. He gets to say he missed it, to mean it even, but he doesn't get to stay.

He never does.

So, I stop thinking.

I tip my hips toward his mouth, chase the pressure, the rhythm, the way he groans like he can't help himself.

I let myself drown in it.

Because if this is all I get—

If this is all we are—

Then at least it'll hurt less when he leaves.

His mouth doesn't falter, not once. He knows my body too well for that, knows the exact pressure to apply, the way to curl his tongue and slip his fingers inside me like he's done it a hundred times before, because, well...he has.

My orgasm hits sharp and fast, a snap of heat behind my eyes, and I come with a gasp that sounds too much like his name.

He doesn't stop right away, draws it out instead—slow and soft now, gentle licks as I ride the wave, like he wants to make sure I feel it. Like he wants to take care.

Like that's not the most dangerous thing he could do.

When I finally go still beneath him, he rests his forehead against my thigh for a second, breathing hard. Then he lifts his head and climbs up the bed toward me.

I expect cocky. I expect smug.

But what I get is careful.

His hand finds my face—just his fingertips brushing along my jaw—and then he kisses me. Slow, deep, messy with affection.

"You okay?" he asks, voice rough.

I blink at him. Then laugh, once—short, breathless, but not because it's funny.

"Don't do that," I say.

His brow furrows. "Do what?"

"Pretend you're checking in on me like this is something it's not."

His hand stills on my cheek.

"I'm not gonna break, Gabe. You don't have to look at me like I'm about to cry or catch feelings or tattoo your name across my ass."

His mouth twitches like he wants to smile, but doesn't.

"I'm fine," I add, sharper this time. "So stop acting like I'm not."

His expression falters, just for a second, that subtle shift in his eyes, the one where he stops being whatever this soft version of him is and slides back into the version I know, the one who knows how to compartmentalize.

"Okay," he says, voice easy again. "You're fine."

"Damn right I am."

He nods, like we've come to some kind of agreement.

I hook my fingers in the waistband of his pants and tug. "Then shut up and fuck me already."

That gets a real smile.

"Thought you'd never ask."

He leans in again, mouth catching mine in a kiss that's hotter now, heavier, like we both just dropped the last of whatever guard we had left.

Only difference is—

He'll pick his back up when this is over.

Mine's already gone.

He kisses me like the conversation didn't just happen, like my deflection didn't cut him, even if I think it might've.

His hands are rougher now—not unkind, just focused. Determined, like he's grateful to have permission to stop pretending this is anything but what I said it is.

His mouth drags down my neck, sucking just hard enough to make me gasp, just hard enough to leave a mark.

My legs part instinctively as he settles between them, and I reach for his belt, fumbling it open without ceremony.

"Need a little help there?" he murmurs, lips brushing my collarbone.

"I swear to God," I mutter, "if you stall for dirty talk, I'll kill you."

He chuckles, low and warm, and kicks off his pants and boxers in one motion, like he's been ready this whole time.

He has.

I can feel it when he presses against me, thick and hot, dragging the head of his cock through the wet mess between my thighs.

We haven't used condoms since that first night.

Afterward, I told him about the IUD. He told me he'd gotten tested a couple months before, and we both agreed to get checked again—just to be sure.

It should've felt clinical. Awkward, maybe.

But, instead, it felt like something else entirely. Like trust, like honesty.

He mentioned once that he never went without protection with

Kara. That even after all those years, something in him still didn't trust her enough to.

But with me? He didn't even flinch.

"You still good?" he asks, voice quieter now. Still rough.

"Gabe," I snap, tugging him closer. "If you ask me that again, I'm gonna walk out of your life and straight into Jackson and Gen's hotel suite."

His laugh stutters, half breath, half groan, as he presses in closer, lining himself up with one hand at my hip.

"Jackson's with your brother tonight," he mutters against my throat. "Y'know, seeing as he and Gen are getting married tomorrow."

I smirk. "Even better. The other side of her bed's empty."

He groans, full-body, the sound punched from somewhere deep.

"Fucking hell, Sage."

And then he thrusts in, slow and thick and shallow—like the joke never happened.

My breath catches, body stretching to take him.

He's still for a beat, forehead pressed to mine, and I can feel the way his fingers flex against my skin, like he's trying to hold it together.

Like if he moves before I tell him to, he'll lose every ounce of self-control he's got left.

And, honestly? I want him to.

The moment stretches, thick with heat and history.

And then—

He thrusts in slow, deep, and all the way.

I suck in a sharp breath, nails digging into his shoulders as he bottoms out.

He holds himself there, buried to the hilt, like he's giving me a second to adjust—or giving himself a second not to lose it.

His forehead rests against mine, breath warm on my mouth.

"Jesus," he mutters. "You feel so fucking good."

I clench around him, just to be a menace. "You gonna move or just lay there like it's a sleepover?"

His laugh is rough, ragged. "You're unbelievable."

But he pulls back, hips rolling once before snapping forward again—and that's all it takes.

My head drops back with a moan I don't stifle in time.

He sets a rhythm, steady and deep, every stroke drawing something out of me I can't hide. The slap of skin on skin echoes, soft and filthy, in the quiet room, the air thick with heat and breath and everything we're not saying.

I wrap my legs around his waist, dragging him in closer, tighter.

"Goddamn, Sage," he groans. "You want all of me or what?"

I bite his shoulder, just enough to leave a mark. "Always have."

It slips out too easily.

His pace falters, just a fraction.

But then he catches it again, hands gripping my hips harder now, like he's chasing the high instead of the meaning.

Good.

So am I.

"Always have," I repeat, but this time it's sharper, a challenge. "You just didn't notice because your head was too far up your own ass."

He groans, fucking into me harder. "Jesus, Sage."

"What?" I pant. "Don't like hearing the truth while you're balls-deep in it?"

His head drops to my shoulder, breath hot. "You're such a pain in the ass."

"And yet," I gasp, rolling my hips up to meet his next thrust, "here you are."

He growls. Actually growls. "Yeah. Here I fucking am."

One hand leaves my hip, slips between us, fingers finding my clit and circling hard enough to make my vision blur.

My mouth falls open. A moan tears from my throat before I can swallow it.

"God, you're so fucking loud," he mutters. "Bet the whole floor can hear you."

"Good," I choke out. "Let them know it's you making me come."

His rhythm stutters—he wasn't ready for that.

But I meant it.

I'm past the point of pretending now.

Because if this is the last time, if this is all I get before he goes back to her, I want it burned into him.

Every sound. Every word. Every part of me he can't unfeel.

"Gabe—" I gasp, head tipping back, "I'm close."

He swears under his breath, rhythm faltering for a second. Then he slows, like he needs to drag it out.

His hips roll deeper, more controlled, every thrust deliberate— like he's pulling me apart one careful inch at a time.

But his hand doesn't stop.

His thumb keeps circling my clit, tight and fast and messy with focus.

"Come on, baby," he murmurs, voice wrecked and shaking. "Let me feel you. I need to feel you."

My whole body arches off the bed, thighs trembling around his waist.

"Gabe—fuck—"

"I've got you," he says, more plea than promise. "Just let go. I've got you."

And I do.

My orgasm rips through me like a snapped wire—hot, frantic, unstoppable.

I clench around him, legs tight around his hips, and that's it, that's all it takes.

He chokes out a sound, raw, desperate, and thrusts once more, deep and hard, before stilling completely.

"Fuck—Sage—"

He groans into my neck as he comes, body shaking, fingers digging into my hip like he's afraid I'll disappear if he doesn't hold on.

I feel every pulse of it inside me. The way he gasps, the way he buries his face in my shoulder, as though the feeling knocked something loose within him.

He doesn't say anything.

Doesn't need to.

His body says it all.

This wasn't casual.

It never was.

And for a second, I almost let myself believe it means something.

But only for a second.

We stay like that for a moment—bodies tangled, skin damp, breath still catching.

I wait for him to roll off me, to give me space, to let me reset.

But he doesn't.

Instead, he shifts just enough to stay inside me as he lowers us both onto the bed, one arm curled around my waist, the other sliding beneath my head like he means to stay.

I try to laugh. Try to wriggle away. "All right, clingy."

"You said something," he says softly, ignoring the dig.

"Yeah," I say, already slipping on the mask again. "It's called pillow talk. Happens in the moment, hormones and all that. Common side effect."

He doesn't laugh. "Sage."

I close my eyes. "Drop it."

"No."

His fingers trace idle shapes along my side, gentle in a way that makes my chest ache. "You said 'always have.' Like...like you meant it."

I shrug, trying to stay casual even though my throat feels tight. "It's a figure of speech. I also said I was gonna sleep with Gen, remember?"

"That was a joke."

"So was this."

He exhales sharply, shifts to look at me. "I'm not with Kara."

I blink up at the ceiling. "Okay."

"I'm not going back to her."

I turn my head, just enough to meet his eyes. There's something real there—something raw enough that it makes it hard to breathe.

"We don't have to stop this," he says, quieter now. "If it's not nothing for you...it's not nothing for me either."

God, I want to believe him.

I want to believe this could actually be different.

So, I nod. Just once. "Okay."

He pulls out before relaxing beside me, drawing me in tighter, wrapping around me like it's instinct.

And for the first time in forever, I let him.

I let myself be held.

Let myself feel like maybe, just maybe, this won't break me.

———

I wake slowly, blinking into the soft morning light filtering through the hotel curtains.

His arm's still around me, his chest pressed to my back.

He stayed.

I should feel good about that, but there's a heaviness in my chest I can't shake.

And then—

Knocking.

Sharp, rapid, urgent.

"SAGE?" Savannah's voice, muffled but unmistakable.

And underneath it—

Gabe's phone ringing.

The name lighting up the screen in bold, unforgiving letters: **Kara**.

I go still.

Gabe doesn't move right away—just groans and buries his face in my neck like he hasn't registered what's happening.

But I already know.

This is the part where everything crashes.

Knocking again, harder this time.

"Sage, open the damn door!"

I jolt upright, heartbeat hammering, and grab the sheet as I shove Gabe's shoulder.

"Get up," I hiss. "Now."

He groans, eyes still half-closed. "What the—"

His phone buzzes again. He glances toward it—blinks once, then twice.

The color drains from his face.

"Seriously?" I snap, wrapping the sheet around myself and stumbling off the bed. "You said you weren't going back to her."

"I'm not," he says automatically, voice rough and guilty. "I— fuck, I didn't know she'd call."

"Yeah, well," I mutter, heading for the door, "she did."

I fling it open.

Savannah stands on the other side, arms crossed, dressed and visibly annoyed.

"There you are," she says, not even bothering with a hello. "You were supposed to be in the bridal suite an hour ago. Gen's panicking about her hair, we can't find the steamer, and you should already be up there."

I blink at her, the sheet pulled tight around my chest, hair a mess, makeup smudged.

Her gaze flicks past me, over my shoulder, to the unmistakable shape of Gabe, sitting on the edge of the bed with the blanket draped over his lap, rubbing a hand down his face like he's still trying to process what the hell he woke up to.

Savannah stares, blinks, then slowly exhales.

"You know what?" she says, holding up a hand. "I'll yell at you later. Right now? Upstairs. Gen needs you."

I nod, swallowing whatever stupid thing I was about to say. "Yeah. Okay."

I move past her without looking back.

Behind me, I hear Gabe's phone buzzing again.

"Give me a minute," he calls after me. "I just need to—"

But I already know what that means.

I hear the balcony door slide open.

I don't wait.

I just walk.

Because I already gave him a minute.

I gave him a night.

And if that didn't change anything...nothing will.

FOUR

PRESENT DAY

GABE

The tall brick apartment building stands unchanged, but it still feels like it's glaring at me.

The bright mums lining the steps, the hanging baskets, the stupidly serene oak tree—they all feel like set dressing for a life that isn't mine yet. One I'm barging into. My grip tightens around the handle of the box I'm carrying, and I pretend the weight in my chest is just the weight of my shit.

I haven't even made it through the door and I already want to turn around.

This morning's phone call with my mom lingers like smoke in my lungs. Her slurred "Just thinking about that time," and the way she still forgets—or refuses to believe—that Kara and I are done. That she always loved Kara more than she ever loved me. That maybe she just loved that Kara made me easier to deal with.

But Sage is the one I have to face now.

I knock, even though I have the key. Wes gave it to me last week with a shrug and a muttered "She'll get over it." He was trying to help. But this feels like walking into enemy territory unarmed.

"One sec!" she calls through the door. A beat later, it swings open, and she stops short when she sees me.

"Oh. It's you."

The smile drops. The whole vibe shifts.

"It's me," I say, trying for neutral.

She narrows her eyes. "Didn't Wes give you a key?"

"He did. It just felt rude to use it."

"Wouldn't be your first time being an asshole," she says, arms crossing over her oversized Braves T-shirt. "So why change it up now?"

I swallow. "I'm sorry."

Her gaze hardens. "Oh? For what?"

"For everything."

It's vague, sure, but it's the truth. I've got a catalog of things I've done wrong, and most of them start and end with her.

She stares at me for a long moment, like she's daring me to flinch, and then turns on her heel and walks back into the apartment without a word.

I step inside slowly, the air thick with everything we're not saying. She sprawls across the couch like she owns the place—which, to be fair, she kind of does—and flips open a magazine. No glance in my direction. No acknowledgment.

Just silence.

I spend the next hour hauling boxes, the strain in my muscles doing nothing to distract from the one behind my ribs. The spare room is bigger than I expected, clean and empty except for a few stray thumbtack holes in the walls and curtains that still smell like Hannah's perfume.

It's nothing, but it's mine now.

I take a long shower, hoping the hot water will wash off more than sweat. It doesn't.

When I walk back out, towel slung low on my hips, Sage is at the stove, stirring something in a pot. Her back is to me, but her shoulders tense the second she hears my footsteps.

She turns, eyes trailing briefly down my chest before darting away again, and I swear I see the faintest flush rise in her cheeks.

"Sage," I say softly. "I meant it. I'm sorry."

She doesn't meet my eyes.

"It doesn't matter," she mutters, voice low and edged with exhaustion. "It happened. It's over. It's never happening again." She turns back to the stove.

I nod, even though she can't see me, and retreat to my room to get dressed.

When I come back out, she's sitting at the kitchen table. A spiral notebook sits open in front of her, a pen in her hand and a look on her face that makes my stomach twist.

"Sit," she says.

I do.

She flips the page and starts writing without preamble, the scratch of her pen loud in the silence. After a few lines, she rips the page out with a clean tug and slides it across the table.

Cohabitation Bible
No sex with roommates
Didn't buy it = don't eat it
Do your dishes
No drama (i.e., no Kara)

"I don't care who you date," she says, voice even. "But Kara is not welcome here. I shouldn't have to feel uncomfortable in my own home."

"She won't be a problem," I say quickly.

Sage doesn't respond. She just stands, walks to the fridge, and pins the rules to the door with a peach-shaped magnet. Her back is rigid, her hands trembling just barely.

"Sage—" I start, but the second I step toward her, she jerks away from me.

"It's the only way this works."

Her voice is barely a whisper. She doesn't wait for a response. She just walks to her room and closes the door behind her.

I stare at the fridge. At the list. At the line between us that now lives in ink.

This was never supposed to get so messy.

But now we're here.

And she's not wrong.

It's the only way this works.

———

For weeks, we've been tiptoeing around each other like ships in uncharted waters, careful not to cross the invisible lines Sage laid down. I hate it. But it's not like I have a long list of housing options right now, and pissing her off feels like a fast track to burning the last bridge I have.

And the thing is—I still want her to forgive me.

Maybe that's delusional. Maybe that chance is already long gone. But until she slams the door for good, I can't help holding onto the flicker of hope that maybe, just maybe, she'll look at me the way she used to. I'm not ready to let that die.

The doorbell rings, loud and jarring, followed by a dramatic round of pounding and a voice singing off-key through the wood.

Liam.

I groan and hurry to the door before he gets bolder. Sure enough, the moment I open it, he grins like a man on a mission and strolls in like he owns the place.

"No, come on in," I deadpan, closing the door behind him.

He's been a walking cloud of gloom lately, so the sudden cheeriness throws me off. I narrow my eyes. "Okay, what's with the musical number? Did you win the lottery? Get laid? Join a cult?"

"Hannah's coming home next week," he says, grinning like he can't help it.

Of course. Hannah Thatcher-Miles—his long-time nemesis-turned-girlfriend. It still trips me out sometimes, how fast that flipped. But he's better for it, happier, lighter. And despite everything, I like seeing him like this.

He launches into a ramble about her tour—some musical, nearly wrapped—and how she'll be back in Atlanta soon. I half-listen, but a selfish thought worms its way to the front of my mind.

"She's not...moving back in here, is she?" I ask, gesturing vaguely around the apartment I just moved into.

Liam barks a laugh. "Here? Hell no. She's moving in with me... or she will be once I talk her into it. Until then, she's crashing at Jackson's."

"Makes sense."

Liam's eyes scan the dim room, taking in the empty furniture and the stillness of the air. "Where's Sage?" he asks, turning to me.

"I think she has a shift at Harry's," I reply honestly. She didn't tell me her plans; she has barely spoken to me in days and disappears without a word. But seeing the familiar Harry's T-shirt on her when she left made me assume.

"How's that going so far?" Liam asks. It's a seemingly innocuous question, but, given how it's been going, I find myself taking the defensive.

"Fine." It comes out a bit snippy.

Liam doesn't typically pry. That has always been one of the reasons our friendship works so well: we don't pry, at least not usually.

"It seems tense." Apparently, today is not the usual.

"Yeah." The hallmark of a one-word answer is that it is usually a not-so-thinly veiled hint to leave the topic alone, but Liam Park doesn't have the same understanding of social clues that the normal person does.

"Did something happen with you guys?"

The question causes me to freeze. It isn't that I make a habit of lying to Liam or withholding information, but this has always been something that Sage and I agreed not to tell people. Primarily because our friend group is far too nosy and neither of us really cares to have our personal lives become brunch talk fodder.

But I don't want to lie, so I say nothing. I just walk toward the kitchen and open the fridge.

"Do you want a drink?" I ask.

Liam's gaze lingers on me for a moment, his expression unreadable. Eventually, he nods and follows me into the kitchen. I grab two bottles of beer and hand one to him, the condensation instantly wetting my palms. As we both take a sip, I can't help but feel grateful for his lack of prodding.

After a few moments of comfortable silence, Liam speaks up again. "You know, you can tell me anything, right? I'm here for you. I know I wasn't exactly supportive when you were with Kara, but that is because we both knew you could do better." His words are gentle, filled with genuine care, which doesn't come as a surprise. I glance up at him, seeing the sincerity in his eyes. I know he cares; that's never been the problem.

I set my bottle down before letting out a sigh and resting my palms against the harsh edge of the countertop. "We fucked." I say it matter-of-factly, but I don't have the energy or interest in sugarcoating what I'm saying.

Liam clearly didn't expect that to come out of my mouth—he chokes on his beer halfway down his throat.

He coughs for about a minute before composing himself, his eyes wide as he stares at me. "I'm sorry, what?"

"Don't play dumb. It's unbecoming of you." I roll my eyes.

"Dude, when?" Liam's shock is palpable, the air heavy with unspoken words.

I take a deep breath, steeling myself before continuing. "It was a few months ago—at least...the last time it happened," I admit, feeling a weight lift off my chest as the truth spills out. "After Gen and Jackson's rehearsal dinner, we both ended up back at her room."

The memories flood back, unwelcome but persistent. I can still taste the bitterness of regret in my mouth. Not for sleeping with Sage—quite the contrary, in fact. She is about the only thing I don't regret, but how I handled it afterward was...horrible.

Liam runs a hand through his hair, his expression a mix of disbelief and concern. "Last time? How many times has that happened?" he asks as his eyes go wide and he searches mine for answers.

"I don't know." I rub my brow, a bit uncomfortable with the forthcoming nature of this conversation. "Half a dozen times, give or take."

Liam lets out a heavy sigh, his shoulders slumping slightly. "Dude, what the fuck," he says, his voice tinged with irritation.

And this is the other reason I didn't want to talk to him about it. He's not just my friend; he's friends with Sage too, and I'm fully aware that despite my intentions not being so, I fucked up.

"I know."

"That's fucked up, man. You cheated on Kara with Sage? While you knew Sage was emotionally involved?"

I don't appreciate the way he assumes I used her, like I must have just wanted to fuck her with little concern. Nor do I like the other implication. "It never happened when Kara and I were together. It was when we'd break up."

"Like that's any better." He scoffs, irritation morphing into anger. "You used her feelings, dude—that's not cool."

I want to tell him that she has never been the only one who

cared. I want to tell him everything, but when I open my mouth, I just say, "I know. I messed up." The confession is barely a whisper. "I never meant for things to spiral out of control like this."

"You need to fix this."

"I'm trying." It comes out reminiscent of a growl, but Liam doesn't back down.

"How?"

"I don't know."

FIVE

SAGE

"Is Brittany coming in tonight?" I ask as I wipe down the lacquered bar top, the beginning of my shift starting in chaos.

From the moment I walked into the bar fifteen minutes ago, I saw Harry, the owner, scrambling behind the bar. He moves around like a bull in a china shop, knocking over bottles and spilling drinks. The dated dive bar sits in the heart of the city, and while there are often lulls in business throughout the week, when it's busy, it's debilitatingly busy for one person—especially someone who can't physically keep up.

His face is flushed and his hands tremble as he attempts to pour a shot of Patrón. He's in his mid-sixties, and his health has visibly declined over the past few months. Brittany must have called off last minute, leaving him to tend the bar alone until I arrived. I wish he'd called—I would have come in early.

"She called off," he mumbles, clearly struggling.

I step toward him and gently take the bottle of tequila from his hands. "I got it." I smile. He's trying, but we all reach a point where we need help.

"No, I've got it. Go get the guy at the other end of the bar."

"No," I say softly, meeting his eyes. "I've got this. I'll grab him after I get this shot to the customer. Who's it for?"

He pauses, then finally lets go of the glass. "The woman in the corner booth."

"Got it. Now, please, go sit down."

Begrudgingly, he steps away. Within minutes, the backlog clears and the pace normalizes. An hour flies by. When there's a break, I slip into the back to check on him.

"Hey, big man, how's it going back here?"

Harry looks up from his desk with weary eyes, the lines on his face deep under the dim light. "It's tough, kid." He sighs. "I've been thinking...maybe it's time to sell the bar."

The words gut me.

"This place is your legacy," I protest. "You can't just give up."

"I appreciate your loyalty, but it's time."

I nod, swallowing my sadness. "If it's what's best for you, I'll support it."

He squeezes my hand and nods. "I want to make sure this place is left in good hands."

I try to smile. "I just hope whoever takes over doesn't ruin what makes this place special." I pause for a moment. "I'm gonna head back out there. Pretty sure drunk strangers behind the bar are a massive liability."

That earns a laugh.

As I make my way back, I hear my name shrieked in a high-pitched voice. Savannah, practically vibrating with excitement, is waving with Gen right beside her. I mix Savannah a mocktail without comment, keeping her secret safe.

Their laughter fills the space, and it reminds me of what makes this place feel like home. Even if it won't be mine forever.

The night moves quickly. Just as I'm wiping down the bar, Gabe walks in.

Perfect.

Wes, Jackson, and Liam follow behind.

"Why is it that you manage to show up here every time I'm working?" I call to Liam.

"The free drinks, obviously."

"I don't give you free drinks."

"Not yet. But if I lay the groundwork now..."

"You're an idiot."

"You love me."

"Like taxes."

Despite the weirdness with Gabe, I can't help but smile. I needed a night like this.

Then Gabe speaks. "Hey, you okay?"

I grit my teeth. "I'm fine."

I busy myself cleaning, trying to ignore the way his gaze lingers. I notice how he leans over the bar, chatting easily with a group of regulars—one of whom has clearly spilled half their beer. To my complete surprise, Gabe grabs a rag from the back counter and wipes it up before I even have to ask. He even helps Harry stack the clean glasses—no prompting, just quietly grabbing and sorting like he's done it before. It's not a big moment. But it's...weirdly thoughtful.

Later, as I'm exiting the kitchen, Savannah corners me with a raised eyebrow and a smirk. "He's not exactly subtle, you know."

I frown. "What are you talking about?"

"Gabe. The cleaning. The helping. The overly convenient 'accidental' coffee refills every morning. I'm just saying, if you want to keep pretending he's not trying, I'm going to start questioning your sanity."

I roll my eyes, but my brain replays the small things. The bathroom sink, wiped down last night. My favorite mug, washed and set out beside the coffee pot. He's trying. I know he is.

This morning, I came out of the shower to find the trash already taken out and the floors swept. The laundry basket that had been half-full was empty—and folded clothes were neatly stacked on the coffee table. There wasn't a note. Just a steaming cup of my favorite coffee waiting on the kitchen counter.

I hadn't known what to do with it; I still don't.

Now, I catch him drying pint glasses behind the bar again, sleeves rolled to his elbows. The way he moves is so damn casual, so familiar, like he belongs here—like he's part of this life I've built for myself.

He glances up and catches me watching him. There's a beat. A flicker of a smile that he doesn't quite let loose.

"See something you like?" he asks, just loud enough for only me to hear.

I blink. My gaze jerks up from where it had, unfortunately, lingered, and his mouth curves into a knowing smirk.

Of course he noticed.

The worst part? For half a second, I liked what I saw.

But desire isn't the same as trust, and a nice forearm doesn't erase a year of emotional whiplash.

I grab a rag from the bar, forcing myself to look unimpressed even as my pulse betrays me.

"You missed a spot."

I try to act like it's nothing, like my pulse isn't thudding with memories I've tried hard to bury, but he leans just a little closer.

"Don't worry, Sage. I'm a quick learner."

God, I hate him.

God, I don't.

Eventually, I step out from behind the bar to get some air. The back alley is quiet, so I lean against the brick wall and tip my head back.

Footsteps crunch behind me.

Of course.

"I didn't mean to push," Gabe says. "You just looked...off."

"I'm not your problem," I mutter.

He doesn't leave. "You've been different," he says after a beat. "I didn't expect...this."

"Well, welcome to consequences."

Something flickers in his expression. He takes a step closer, then stops. "I've been trying," he says. "Around the apartment. I thought maybe—"

"Trying doesn't erase what already happened."

He swallows, and I can tell he wants to say something more. Instead, he just nods.

I brush past him to go back inside. As I reach for the door handle, I hear him quietly say, "I'm sorry."

I pause but don't turn around.

Because I remember the last time he said that.

Back in the bar, I shake off the memory like a drop of cold water.

Savannah catches my eye from her booth. "Like I said, not subtle," she mouths.

I roll my eyes and turn back to the bar, leaving Gabe's gaze behind me.

Because I'm not doing this again.

Not with him.

SIX

GABE

"She doesn't hate you," Liam says with an almost-laugh as he sits across from me at Andre's, the mocking nature of his amusement at my vulnerability precariously perched on the edge of pissing me the fuck off.

"Oh, but she does."

"No—she doesn't. Trust me, I'd know."

"And how would you know that?"

"You mean other than the fact that we've had this conversation *ad nauseam* about me and Hannah?"

"Hannah *did* hate you." I roll my eyes before taking a sip of my soda.

"Doesn't matter, because she didn't really hate me. It was complicated. You and Sage, complicated. But she doesn't hate you."

I want to think he's right—that this is just where we're at, that being roommates has the potential to mend the damage I've done, that maybe we can get back to a place of friendship. But...I screwed up, colossally. If I were Sage, I don't know if I would forgive me.

Sometimes, intentions stop mattering if the damage happens anyway.

"We're not you and Hannah. You and Hannah had a lot more tying you to one another. Sage could choose tomorrow that she doesn't want me in her life, and the only thing preventing that from being true is that we now live together."

Liam lets out a groan before leaning forward in his seat and steepling his fingers in front of him. "Gabe?"

"What?" I snip.

"Sage is one of the most compassionate people I know. And for only God knows what reason, she clearly has a boundless capacity to forgive you specifically."

I don't think Liam realizes that I believe she's found that boundary.

"I don't know."

"Just try, man. I know it sounds crazy, but it's just crazy enough to maybe work. Try, put in effort. Be the good guy I know you can be. Also, block Kara."

"I haven't been talking to Kara."

"I don't care. She always manages to reel you back in, and if she does, you will lose Sage. She can say all she wants that she doesn't care who you date, and who knows, maybe she doesn't. But if you guys are going to work as roommates, it can't be Kara."

"I get it."

"Good." He takes a sip of his drink before leaning back in his seat, his previous serious demeanor shifting into amusement. "Now, let's get back to the important topic here. Me."

"You're so humble."

"Never claimed to be."

We leave Andre's an hour later, full of burgers and unsolicited advice. We return to my place, where Liam becomes fully entrenched in a high-speed police chase.

Liam pushes down with the pad of his thumb, pressing the joystick flush with the controller as he barrels through the street in a game of *Grand Theft Auto*. I'm just glad that, amidst our many fights, Kara didn't break my PS5 in a fit of rage.

Silver linings, I guess.

As Liam skillfully navigates through the virtual city streets, I can't help but marvel at his focus. His eyes are narrowed in concentration, his fingers moving fluidly over the controller buttons. The sounds of screeching tires and police sirens fill the room, causing the game to thankfully be the only thing I can focus on.

I lean back on the couch as I pull my soda to my lips, just relieved to have a moment where I'm not stressing over someone else's bullshit.

Except, well...Liam's.

Suddenly, a loud crash echoes through the game as his character careens into a police car, sending it spinning out of control. We both burst into laughter as Liam drops the controller onto the coffee table before grabbing his can of Sprite off the glass top and bringing it to his mouth.

My phone dings against the cold glass and I instantly move to grab it until I notice the name spelled out across the screen.

Kara.

I was hoping to avoid any contact with her. She had been out when I came to pick up my remaining belongings last week, and she hadn't reached out since then. While there have been brief moments of concern, I have been mostly thankful for a period of abject peace.

Until now, that is.

"You just said you're done with her. Are you seriously talking to her again?" Liam's irritation slips through the air, pulling me out of my daze as I stare down at my iPhone with a blank expression. I shake my head, both in response and to dislodge whatever adverse effect seeing her name across my screen caused.

"Of course not," I say before reaching for the controller, but

Liam just yanks it out of my reach. "Dude, I'm serious. I haven't spoken to her."

"Then why is she texting you?" His concern is palpable, but irritating as hell.

"Why, you jealous?" I try to make light of it with a joking wink, but his scowl only grows.

He stares at me for another beat before letting out a sigh. "Gabe, you can't keep doing this with her. It's not healthy."

"Like I said, I'm not." I reach over and grab the controller from his grasp. My fingers wrap tightly around the plastic as I try to distract myself from the constant buzzing in front of me, my phone notifying me a second time about the text messages. Sitting innocently on the coffee table, it seems to taunt me with its unread message notifications. My eyes flicker toward it, but I quickly avert my gaze, knowing that if I pick it up, I won't be able to resist checking the messages.

Liam's attention is still locked on my phone, as if he expects it to explode at any moment like a ticking time bomb. His expression is a mix of curiosity and concern, and I can feel his silent questions burning into my skin.

"Are you going to read it?" he finally asks, breaking the tense silence between us.

I hesitate, my mind racing with conflicting thoughts and emotions. Part of me doesn't want to read it, afraid of what it might say or how it might make me feel. But another part of me, a nagging voice deep inside, urges me to pick up my phone and read the message. What if something happened to her? What if she needs me?

It wouldn't be the first time she ended up in the hospital after a breakup like this. The last time we went through a breakup that lasted this long, she ended up in the hospital. I remember getting a call from her mother, explaining how she had "accidentally" overdosed on medication. Even though it was an accident, I couldn't help but wonder if our relationship troubles played a part in her actions.

As much as I try to push away these haunting memories and fears, they continue to linger in the back of my mind, gnawing at me like a persistent itch that can't be scratched.

Because every time Kara cried or clung or threatened to break if I left, all I could see was my mother—fragile and furious, manipulative in the name of love. Maybe that's why they were always so close.

"You good, man?" Liam's tone quickly shifts from accusatory to concerned, and while it makes me exceedingly grateful to have a best friend who cares, I also don't want to talk about it.

"Yeah, I'm good," I respond before shifting to grab my phone off the table, taking a deep breath, and opening the text message thread.

> KARA
>
> Can we talk?
>
> Please?

We've been here before, the pleading part. The part where she attempts to appeal to my concern for her, or just tries to make herself not come off as damaging as she can be. It's exactly how it went last time. This cycle, this shit with her, it's been years of it. And while I care about her, want what's best for her, and don't want anything bad to happen to her, I am exhausted. Not the kind of exhaustion that one feels after a long day at work, but the kind of bone-deep exhaustion that even sleeping for ten days straight can't shake you out of.

Despite every instinct in my body pushing me to answer her, just to confirm that she is indeed okay, I block her number, then click my phone screen off and put it on silent.

An odd, triumphant feeling consumes me, and instantly, I am reminded of just how pathetic that is.

After several intense rounds of video games, Liam finally speaks up. His voice breaks the tense silence that has been hanging between us for hours.

"So, how's living with Sage?" he asks.

I shoot him a look. "You don't have to ask me that constantly."

He grins mischievously. "But I can't help it. I'm still amazed she hasn't killed you yet."

I immediately regret telling him about hooking up with Sage. Liam may be my best friend, but he has a habit of bringing up things I'd rather not talk about.

"Me too," I reply casually, trying to brush off the topic. Just then, I hear the sound of keys jingling in the lock and the doorknob turning. Without even looking toward the door, I can tell it's Sage. But before she steps inside, Liam jumps up from the couch and shouts out her name with far too much enthusiasm.

"Sage! You're just in time. We were just talking about you," Liam announces, flashing a sly grin in my direction. I shoot him a warning glance, but he just winks back at me. Leave it to him to make things weird on purpose.

Sage enters the room, her eyes flickering between the two of us. "Oh really? I hope it was all good things," she says with a smirk, setting her keys down on the table. The playful nature is something I miss about her, something I don't see anymore. It used to be like that with us; we used to joke and play around with one another—until I up and ruined everything.

"Of course, always good things," Liam chimes in before I can respond.

I roll my eyes. Liam can be such a suck-up when he wants to be. But Sage just laughs, her easy demeanor a breath of fresh air until her eyes meet mine and her face instantly falls.

She clears her throat and shifts her gaze away, a tense silence settling in the room. Liam seems to pick up on the discomfort and stands abruptly, announcing that Hannah is calling despite his phone not making a sound. As soon as he exits, Sage walks over to where I'm sitting, perching on the arm of the couch next to me.

Progress. Or, at least, I'm going to convince myself it's progress.

"How was work?" I ask, not looking up at her, not wanting to startle her out of whatever semblance of pleasantry this is.

"It was fine." She lets out a sigh, making it abundantly clear that it was anything but fine. But do I ask about it?

I don't know the rules—I don't know how I'm supposed to handle this. We're in uncharted territory, and for the first time since I met this girl, I find it hard to look at her.

I just nod in response.

To my surprise, amidst the lingering silence, she continues. "The last few shifts have kinda sucked. Harry is talking about selling. And you know as well as I do that some chain is probably going to swoop in and make an offer; he's in too prime of a spot. Then it'll just be...gone."

I try and fail to quell my excitement at her willingness to talk to me, *really* talk to me, but thankfully she doesn't comment on it.

"Well, why don't you buy the bar?" I ask in an offhand tone, mostly in an effort to continue the conversation.

Sage lets out a sardonic laugh, as if the mere thought of her owning a business is lunacy. "Yeah, right. Good one, Gabe."

Okay, I don't like *that.* "Why is that laughable? I know you have a trust—it's not like you don't have the money."

"In what world do *I* seem the business owner type?" Despite her resistance to the topic, I watch her mull it over.

I hate that she doesn't think she could do this. I've watched her ever since she started working at Harry's. I've watched as she's come alive working behind that bar. I know that she holds firm that her career isn't her purpose, but that doesn't mean something couldn't come along that could change that for her. Give her something new to love.

And I know she does love it. She loves working at Harry's, yes, but she lights up when she's talking to people there. Asking them about their lives, learning about their different paths. It's a community, one to which Sage has become central.

Silence lingers in the air as she bites her inner cheek, and I fight off every desire to further encourage her to do this. She's never been the type to listen to others about what she should do; she's infallible in that way, and she needs to come to that decision on her own.

She truly is unlike any human being I've ever known.

Just when I've mustered the confidence to barrel through the quiet, the doorknob of the front door twists and Liam reappears in the doorway, sweat dripping down his neck.

"Jeez, man, did you go for a run?" Sage peers up at him in amusement, her eyes lingering on his sweat-dampened skin.

"I don't want to talk about it." He seems frazzled.

My lips turn upward as I realize—a beehive recently popped up outside the door.

"You got chased by a bee, didn't you?"

"I said *I don't want to talk about it!*"

Sage and I burst into laughter as Liam huffs away into the kitchen, clearly helping himself without a care in the world.

This is what I wanted; this is what I was hoping for when I moved in with Sage.

Of course, there's part of me that wishes we could be more, that wishes I could go back and redo everything—go back and not hurt her the way I did. Go back and not get back together with Kara again. But if we can get back to a place where we can genuinely be friends, hang out without the tension, spend time together because we genuinely want to and not because we've been forced to share an apartment...I could learn to be okay with just that.

Happily.

Liam hangs out at the apartment for a few more hours, and, despite claiming he isn't losing his ever-loving mind about Hannah returning tomorrow, I know he is. The person that he has slowly become by loving Hannah has been equal parts terrifying and extraordinary to watch. He was never the type of guy to want that—to be in a relationship that consumes him—but I guess he was always holding out for it to be Hannah.

As I watch Sage throw her head back in laughter, a tight ringlet falls across her face. She reaches up to tuck it behind her ear, and my heart races at the simple gesture. It's been this way since the day I met her—every time I see her, I feel like I'm losing control.

But the thought of being with Sage, truly being with her, would mean letting go of all my fears and insecurities. It could be the most exhilarating experience of my life, or it could destroy me completely. And yet, I can't help but crave it more than anything else in this world.

I never let myself want that—this, *her*—but as I look at her right now, I can't envision my life any differently.

My stomach plummets as I remember...she's done.

The apartment went quiet when Liam left hours ago, claiming he had "packing to do" for Hannah's arrival, but I think he just didn't want to be in the middle of whatever it is Sage and I are—or aren't.

I linger in the kitchen longer than I need to. Load the dishwasher even though half the stuff's already clean. Wipe down the counter again, try not to think about how she looked tonight when she laughed. Or the way she didn't look back when I told her I was sorry.

Her bedroom door's still closed.

I don't know what I expect when I knock. A fight, maybe. Silence. But the soft shuffle of feet followed by the click of the door unlatching catches me off guard.

She doesn't open it all the way—just leans in the frame, hoodie tugged around her, curls a little frizzy after her long shift.

Her expression is unreadable. "What?"

"I didn't say it right last night," I tell her. "At the bar."

Sage sighs and leans her shoulder against the frame. She doesn't close the door. Doesn't open it more, either.

"You don't have to forgive me," I say before I can talk myself out of it. "I wouldn't if I were you. But I'm not leaving unless you tell me to."

Something flickers across her face—something that softens, just barely, before it hardens again. "You always say the right thing," she says. "Doesn't mean you mean it."

"I know," I admit. "That's why I'm not trying to convince you anymore. I'm just gonna keep showing you."

Sage stares at me for a long time. The silence stretches, heavy and fragile all at once.

And then, with a sigh, she steps back and lets the door fall shut.

Not slammed. Not locked.

Just...closed.

SEVEN

SAGE

The bar smells like burnt citrus and old fryer oil.

That's how I know it was a bad night. When the scent lingers on my skin like it's trying to remind me of everything I couldn't fix.

Harry didn't even yell; that was the worst part.

He just stood there with this vacant look, like he'd already decided to let it all go. Said he was tired, said maybe it's time, that some big chain came sniffing around again and maybe he'll finally say yes.

I think I nodded, I think I said something supportive, like, "Do whatever's best for you."

But I don't remember—my chest was too tight to breathe right.

I didn't intend to get so emotionally attached to a damn bar. And it's not even a nice bar—it's not like it's some top-level-of-a-fancy-hotel, $22-well-liquor-cocktails kind of bar.

It's a dive bar that's been open for decades with hardly any renovations since it opened.

And still, I love it just the same.

Ain't that a kick in the dick.

Now I'm standing in the dark kitchen, keys still clutched in my fist like I forgot to put them down. The fridge hums. There's a flicker in the hallway light, like even the apartment's given up.

And Gabe—

He's sitting at the kitchen table, some half-eaten takeout in front of him and that furrow between his brows that means he's trying to figure out if I'm about to lose it or bite his head off.

I hang my keys on the hook, kick off my boots like it's any other night.

"Hey," he says quietly.

I shrug off my jean jacket. "Hey."

There's a pause—not awkward, not tense. Just...full.

"You hungry?"

"Nope."

"You sure? I saved you—"

"I said I'm fine."

It comes out sharper than I mean for it to, but I don't take it back. I can't; if I soften now, I'll fall apart, and he doesn't *deserve* to see me fall apart.

Gabe nods and looks down at his food, like it suddenly matters more than whatever's happened between us. Like he knows not to poke the bear.

I move to the fridge and open it. Though I'm not going to eat, I just need something to do with my hands. I grab a bottle of water and stare at it like it might tell me what the hell I'm supposed to do next.

When I turn back around, he's still watching me. Not pushing. Just...*there*, like he's been for weeks.

That's what breaks me.

Not the bad night, not Harry giving up.

Not the fact that I might lose the one place that's felt like mine in years.

It's Gabe—sitting there like a goddamn constant, hell-bent on proving he's not the asshole he's been in the past. Like he's really changed, like he's really done with the bullshit, just asking me if I'm hungry as if the world isn't falling apart.

My chest lurches.

"I think he's really gonna sell it," I say, my voice cracking halfway through.

And just like that, I'm crying. Quiet at first, then ugly. Full-body, hands-over-my-face, shoulders-shaking kind of crying.

I don't cry very often. It's not that I can't, but I'm not a generally emotional person, so on the occasion I do, it's typically in front of family, and most definitely *never* in front of Gabe.

That's what makes what happens next so unbearable.

I turn toward the sink, away from him, swiping at my cheeks like that'll fix anything. My shoulders shake harder the more I try to stop them, and my throat tightens with every breath I try to swallow.

Behind me, I hear the chair slide back.

"Sage..."

His footsteps are quiet, careful. I feel him at my back before he touches me.

And then—he does. One hand grazes my arm, and I flinch.

"Don't," I whisper. "I don't need—just—don't."

But he steps closer anyway.

His arms come around me like he's done it a thousand times before. Like it's the most natural thing in the world. I freeze. My hands stay clenched at my sides, and my whole body goes stiff, resisting it.

"Don't," I say again, sharper now. "I said I'm fine."

"You're not," he says, voice low, against the crown of my head.

I shake him off—or try to, at least. He doesn't let go.

Instead, he tightens his grip—not forceful, just...sure. Steady.

And then, in the softest voice I've ever heard from him, he mumbles into my hair, "Let me hold you."

Everything in me rebels against it. Against him.

Because if I let this happen, if I let *him* happen, I don't know if I'll be able to shut it off again.

This isn't what we do anymore. This isn't safe.

My jaw tightens. My fingers twitch at my sides, itching to shove him away, to reclaim the distance I've spent months rebuilding. He doesn't get to comfort me. He doesn't get to show up like this now, all gentle and quiet and good.

But his arms stay steady, warm, familiar in a way that's worse than anything else.

And I hate it—hate how my chest caves in, how my shoulders start to shake harder, how it doesn't matter how much I try to resist this because my body's already making the choice for me.

Slowly, like I'm surrendering to something I don't want to name, I sink into him.

His chest presses to my back, arms wrapping fully around my waist now, and I let my head tip forward, eyes burning as I stare down at the sink.

He doesn't speak, doesn't move, just breathes with me. Slow, quiet, steady, like if he can anchor me long enough, maybe I won't drift off the edge.

My hands lift, unsure, and hover for a second before resting lightly on his forearms. I don't grip him, I don't pull him closer, but I don't push him away, either.

God, I'm so tired of pretending I don't want this, of pretending I don't want him.

His chin brushes the top of my head as he leans down just enough to breathe in the scent of my curls, and it's stupid how much that ruins me.

"I hate you for knowing exactly how to handle me," I whisper, voice hoarse.

He exhales softly, his breath skimming the crown of my head. "I don't. Not really."

"You do," I murmur. "You always have...and that's the problem."

There's a long pause. His grip doesn't change, but I can feel the way his chest rises tighter against my back, my head now resting there. Like he's holding something in—words, feelings, maybe the urge to ruin this and take more.

"Sage," he says, low and wrecked. "You don't have to pretend with me."

The words land like a bruise.

Because that's exactly what I've always had to do with him: pretend I didn't care, pretend it was fine when he'd pull me close one night and vanish the next. Pretend it didn't gut me when he went back to Kara, again, and again, and again.

He never cheated on her, I'll give him that. His moral compass was just intact enough to keep him from crossing that line.

But why didn't it extend to me?

Why wasn't *breaking me slowly* a line he wouldn't cross?

I told him it was just sex. I always said the right things. *Don't worry about it, Gabe. It's fine, I'm fine.*

But I wasn't fine. And if he had looked, really looked, he would've known that.

Hell, I think he did.

That's what makes it worse.

Because even then, he let it happen—let me pretend while he did the same, and we both called it honesty.

Now he wants to play the version of himself that means well, that's trying.

And I want so badly to believe him.

But part of me still burns from the last time I did, when he told me that night while he held me in bed that they were really done, for good this time. And despite the half-dozen times he'd told me that already, for some reason, that night I believed him.

I wanted to believe him.

So I did.

I let myself fall into him that night—not just my body, but *me.*

The part of me that swore I wouldn't do this again, that I could keep it casual, that I wasn't still hoping.

But hope's a slippery thing; it doesn't feel like weakness until you're choking on it.

And the next day...she was at the wedding. With him, on his arm. Wearing that nauseatingly smug smile, like she knew—like she always knew I was just the stand-in for the in-between.

He didn't even look at me when they walked in, or maybe he did and I just couldn't meet his eyes.

Because if I did, I would've shattered. Right there in front of everyone.

I left right after the speeches, said I wasn't feeling well.

And I meant it.

Because I've never felt so fucking humiliated in my life.

Sav could tell I was upset, and, given that she found him in my hotel room that morning, I know she knew why.

I'm just really glad she never brought it up again.

So, yeah—when he says, *"You don't have to pretend with me,"* all I want to do is laugh, or scream, or kiss him so hard he forgets how many times he made me feel like a second choice.

Instead, I breathe.

One shaky inhale, one long exhale.

And then I turn.

His hands shift with me, sliding to my waist like they never left.

He doesn't move closer, doesn't speak. Just watches me—quiet, careful, like he knows he's standing on the edge of something he has no right to hope for.

I hate how much that hurts, how much I still want him, even after everything. How badly I want to feel better, to shut my brain off. And I hate how I know in my gut he's the only one who can do that.

My fingers twitch at my sides. Then I reach for him—grab the front of his shirt in both fists and yank him down, closing the distance myself.

His breath stutters, and his hands flex against my hips, like he's ready to catch me and let go at the same time.

And that's when he says it.

"You sure about this?"

His voice is rough, small, like he already knows I'm not.

I look up at him, my voice sharp even though it's quiet. "Don't look at me like that, just touch me."

He blinks, caught off guard by the venom in my tone.

"And you don't have to pretend it means something," I add, because I can't stop myself. "We both know that's never been your strong suit."

That lands, hard.

He goes still.

I see it—how the words knock the breath out of him for half a second before he swallows it down, shoving the reaction somewhere deep behind his eyes. He doesn't defend himself, doesn't argue. Just nods once, because he knows I'm right.

But his grip on my waist tightens.

And when he leans in, it's with a heat that's laced with guilt. A hunger that tastes like punishment.

Exactly what I wanted, exactly what I asked for.

And when he kisses me again, it's not soft or searching. It's bracing, like he's ready for the weight of this.

I drag him down by the collar of his shirt, mouth crashing into his. There's nothing careful about it. I bite his bottom lip, not hard enough to draw blood, but enough to make him feel.

He exhales heavily, a sound caught between a groan and a curse, and I chase it like I want to bottle it.

My fingers tangle in his hair, nails scraping just a little too roughly at the nape of his neck.

And he lets me—doesn't flinch, doesn't stop me.

His hands are everywhere now—spanning my ribs, my thighs, sliding under my clothes—like he needs to memorize what used to feel like his to touch.

But I don't want tenderness.

Not now, not ever again with him.

So, when his lips skim too gently along my jaw, I pull his head back by his hair, forcing him to look at me.

His eyes are wide, mouth parted, chest heaving like he knows what this is.

"Don't be careful with me," I say.

His voice is ragged when he answers. "I'm not."

And he proves it—dragging my Harry's hoodie up and off, pushing it over my head like he's done it before. I yank his shirt up with the same urgency, needing skin, needing heat, needing friction.

This isn't about love; this isn't even about like.

This is about the ache that's lived under my ribs since the night he left me standing in that hotel hallway, pretending I didn't care.

I sure as hell won't make that mistake again.

I lift onto my toes slightly as I press my mouth to his collarbone, bite hard enough to make him hiss, and drag my teeth along his skin as I move lower. Not sweet, not reverent, just present.

He pulls me closer, hands splaying across my back.

His jeans press tight between my thighs, but I don't grind down —I reach between us and cup him through the denim, squeezing just enough to make him groan.

"Fuck, Sage..." It slips out like he didn't mean to say it, like it was torn from him.

"Shut up." I don't mean it to be cruel; I just can't hear him say my name like that. Not when it sounds like he means it.

Something shifts in him.

The apology that's been hiding behind his eyes—he lets it go, along with the restraint.

He exhales hard before his mouth finds my throat, his hands suddenly everywhere—waist, hips, under my thighs—and then I'm airborne for a second, legs tightening around him as he lifts me onto the counter behind us, right next to the sink.

My back hits the cold tile wall, but I barely register it, because his hands are already on my face, framing it like I'm breakable even now, right before he kisses me so deeply it's almost violent in how full it is. No hesitation, no pretense.

His teeth catch my bottom lip and bite—not hard, not cruel, just enough to match the pressure I gave him earlier. A mirror, a promise. His hands slip down my sides, gripping my hips like he's afraid I'll vanish if he doesn't anchor me there.

I tug at his hair again, harder this time, and he groans into my mouth. I swallow it, chasing that sound like it's mine to claim, because right now...it is.

Clothes become a blur—fingers dragging fabric, pulling, pushing, until we're bare enough that it stops mattering who started what.

He lines up against me, the head of him thick and hot between my thighs, and he pauses only long enough to meet my gaze.

No words, no second chances.

Just the fire we built between us.

Then he pushes in with a groan that rattles through both of us.

I gasp, hand flying to his shoulder, nails sinking in as he stretches me open, inch by inch.

"Jesus," he grits out against my neck.

I bite down on his shoulder, not bothering to muffle the noise that escapes my throat.

His pace stutters, just a little, as his mouth moves toward my ear.

"I missed this..." His words match his thrusts, breathy, like he didn't mean to say it out loud. His voice is wrecked. Wrecking me. "Missed the feel of you. Missed you."

I freeze for half a second, heart thudding too hard.

No.

No, he doesn't get to say that.

I pull back just enough to catch his mouth and kiss him hard—then bite his lip. This time, I don't hold back, not fully.

There's a faint taste of iron. His breath hitches, and he pulls away, blinking down at me like he's trying to figure out if it was an accident.

It wasn't.

He licks his bottom lip before swiping his thumb across his mouth, seeing the blood.

He pauses, but just for a second, and then he crashes back into me.

His lips find mine again, deeper this time, more desperate. I taste the metallic tang of him, us, for just a moment before it disappears completely.

And then he moves.

Frantic, uncontrolled. *Unhinged.*

His hips slam into mine with a force that steals the breath from my lungs, again and again.

I clutch at him, nails digging into his back, his shoulders—anywhere I can hold onto, as if it'll keep me grounded through the onslaught.

But I'm already gone.

Every thrust punches a moan from my throat, louder than I mean to be, borderline screaming now, each cry ripped from me like a confession.

And still, he doesn't stop.

"Fuck," he breathes against my mouth, his voice broken. "You feel—God, Sage—"

I shut him up with another kiss, sloppy and open and wild.

My body is fire and ache and too much all at once. Pressure builds so fast I barely register it; I only know I'm shaking, hips chasing his with a rhythm I can't control.

He groans my name again, and this time I let it slide, let him have it.

Because whatever this is, it's not forgiveness.

And I'm so close to falling over the edge that I can't bring myself to care.

His hand grips the back of my neck, the other steadying us at my hip, and he buries his face against my jaw, breath hot, words nearly choked.

"Please—fuck, please let me feel you come."

I whimper, because *God.*

"I miss it," he says, voice wrecked, thrusts getting sloppier. "The way you fall apart, the way you clench around me like you don't want to let go."

It's filthy, desperate, unforgivable.

And it undoes me.

Heat coils low in my stomach, tight and blinding. Every nerve sparks under my skin as my body goes taut.

"Let me have it," he grits out, mouth against my throat. "I need it, Sage. I need *you.*"

And I break.

Shattering around him with a cry that borders on a sob, my entire body convulsing as the orgasm rips through me, raw, violent, overwhelming.

He groans, loud, guttural, as I clamp down around him, and I barely register his rhythm faltering, the way his whole body tenses as he follows me over the edge with a growl against my skin.

And then, silence.

Nothing but the sound of our breathing.

Harsh. Shallow. And, unfortunately...real.

EIGHT

GABE

We're in the middle of a heat wave, the kind that makes the air inside feel thick no matter how high the AC is cranked. I offered to install a second fan in the living room yesterday—Sage didn't say no, but she didn't say yes either. Just nodded once and kept scrolling through her phone like I wasn't there.

That's been the theme lately.

She doesn't ignore me, not exactly. It's worse than that. She's polite. Efficient. Cordial, even. Like a stranger you thank for holding the elevator door.

I still make dinner most nights, still do the dishes, still take out the trash before she can think to. And I keep showing up at Harry's on her longest shifts—not because she asks, not because she notices, but because someone has to.

She doesn't thank me, doesn't need to.

I'm not doing it for gratitude.

I'm doing it because I want to stay.

Because I want to earn back her trust.

Contrary to popular belief, I'm not an idiot; I know what I did to her was fucked up, and I didn't just do it once. I kept doing it—so it's no surprise she'd recoil after what happened between us last week.

I just...wish she didn't.

I wish she'd talk to me. Hell, I wish I'd just done the right thing in the first place—left Kara when I should have, danced with Sage and only Sage at Jackson and Gen's wedding.

But I didn't. I got back together with Kara; I kept choosing the easier path. I didn't have the backbone to leave her, not when she needed me in ways that felt more like obligation than love.

So now I vacuum the couch.

Not because it needs it, but because I keep hoping that maybe, just maybe, if I do enough, she'll look at me and smile.

The vacuum hums low as I push it across the worn cushions, the brush head lifting flecks of lint and crumbs from between the seams. It's not messy, not really. I cleaned it yesterday. But I'm back at it anyway—because movement feels better than stillness, and because I'm a pathetic glutton for whatever scraps of peace I can earn.

It's sage-green, the couch.

Soft corduroy, slightly faded in the middle where she curls up with a blanket on slow mornings.

Same shade as her name, which feels cruel in a poetic kind of way.

I'm still dragging the vacuum hose along the edge of the armrest when I hear the jangle of keys in the lock. The front door clicks open, and she steps inside, tossing her keys in the ceramic bowl by instinct.

Sage kicks off her shoes one at a time, shoulders slumped, curls frizzed at the crown like she's had them piled in a hair tie all day and yanked it out in the car. Her shirt's wrinkled. She looks tired, and beautiful, and not at all like someone who wants to see me.

I turn the vacuum off, the silence that follows a little too loud.

"You don't have to do that," she says, not unkind, but distant.

Like she's commenting on the weather, or a neighbor's dog barking too early in the morning.

I shrug. "Didn't have anything better to do."

She doesn't respond. Just walks past me into the kitchen, pulling the fridge open like it wronged her.

And for a second, I think that maybe this is the most we'll say all day.

Then, without turning around, she asks, "You want a beer?"

I blink. "Yeah. Sure."

She disappears behind the open fridge door for a second longer —then walks back into the living room and holds out a Sweetwater 420.

I take it from her, careful not to let our fingers brush.

It's not a peace offering.

Not exactly.

But it's something.

And right now, I'll take something.

I crack the can open with a soft hiss and nod toward the barstool she just passed. "Long day?"

She drops onto the arm of the couch instead, tipping her own beer back before answering. "Fryer's acting up again. Katie called off. Couple of regulars wouldn't stop asking if Harry's dying."

I wince. "Want me to look at the fryer?"

She raises an eyebrow, skeptical. "Since when do you fix fryers?"

"I don't," I admit, taking a sip. "But I'm willing to try."

It's not a smile she gives me, not really. But the corner of her mouth twitches like she's considering it.

And for now, I'll take that too.

Quiet settles between us, the kind that hums, low and steady, as though waiting for someone to break it, for *us* to break.

Sage drags her thumb along the rim of the can, then starts flicking the tab back and forth—click, click, click.

"That chain called again, the one I said was sniffing around Harry's," she says finally. "Clover & Oak. They upped their offer."

She doesn't look at me, just keeps flicking the tab like the motion might hold her together.

"Sounds like Harry's gonna take it."

She lifts the can and takes a long gulp—like she's trying to wash the words back down before they settle bitter against her tongue.

I watch her throat work as she swallows, the way her jaw tenses like the beer tastes worse now that it's paired with reality.

"That what you want?" I ask, voice low.

She shrugs, still not looking at me. "Doesn't matter what I want."

"Sage."

She exhales through her nose, sharp and tired, then finally meets my gaze. "I don't know, Gabe. Okay? I don't know what I want. I've worked there longer than I've ever stayed anywhere, which I know isn't much compared to some of you guys, but I've never wanted to stay in one place like that before. Harry's is not just a job, it's..." Her fingers tighten around the can. "It's been the closest thing I've had to a constant. It's the only thing I didn't fuck up."

"You didn't fuck this up either," I say, the words escaping before I can stop them.

Her eyes shutter a little. "I didn't claim to fuck it up," she mutters, dragging the back of her hand across her forehead. "I just...wish he was up for keeping things the same. Not selling, not yet."

I lean forward, elbows braced on my knees. "Sage, he's getting old."

"You think I don't know that?" Her voice spikes as she jolts upright, arms flinging out. "Of course I know that, Gabe! I know! I just—God, I know it's selfish, okay? I'm a deeply selfish person. I want the bar to stay the same, I want Harry to stay the same, I want to walk in and not feel like everything's slipping through my fucking fingers."

She flails again, like the motion will shake the truth loose from her chest.

I don't let her spiral.

"You're not selfish," I say calmly. "And even if you were—this? Wanting something that matters to you to stay? That's not selfish. It's just...impossible."

Her shoulders drop a little, but the fire in her eyes stays lit.

Honestly? I'd rather see that than the numbness.

She sits back down, slower this time, the fight still in her but losing steam. The can sweats between her fingers as she takes another sip, then sets it down on the coffee table with a soft thud.

I watch her for a second longer before I say it—again.

"You know you could buy it."

She exhales hard through her nose. "You already said that."

"I meant it then, and I still do."

"Well, don't." Her voice is flat now, more defense than heat. "Even if Harry would sell it to me—which, again, feels like a long shot—I'm not exactly known for my follow-through. Ask Wes. He's practically got a slideshow presentation on it. Every time I try something new, or change my mind, he's there to remind me. 'That's Sage. Free spirit, never sticks to one thing.'"

She flicks the tab on her can again and adds, "It's not like I've ever been career-driven. I've just...I don't know. I like doing things. Seeing things."

"That's what I love about you."

Her head snaps toward me, eyes narrowing—not angry, just startled, and wary.

I keep going, gently. "You've never chased a title or a paycheck. You've always chased experiences. You're hell-bent on living the fullest fucking life possible, even if it means working as a human statue outside the art museum."

Her mouth twitches, fighting a smile. "That was for, like...two weeks."

"But you did it," I say, shrugging. "Most people would never even think to do that. You have stories, Sage. You have memories people spend their whole lives wishing they were brave enough to make. That's not flaky; that's fearless."

She blinks, then takes another sip—slower this time. When she sets the can down again, her voice is quieter. "Still not buying the bar."

But she doesn't say it with the same finality. It sounds less like a decision and more like a shield. And I don't push, even though I want to. Because I know her well enough to recognize when something's cracking open.

The apartment is too quiet.

Not in a bad way, necessarily, just in a "this is new" kind of way. The TV hums in the background, some reality show neither of us is really paying attention to, and there's a half-empty takeout spread on the coffee table. I'm curled into the far end of the couch with my legs tucked under me, balancing a carton of noodles in one hand and my chopsticks in the other.

Gabe's at the other end, one ankle propped on the opposite knee, flipping through sauce packets like he's conducting an interview.

We haven't said much since we got home. A few comments about traffic, an offhand remark about the dumplings. Laughter, quiet and quick, over something dumb someone said on TV. It's the most normal night we've had...ever?

Except, it's not normal.

The equilibrium is off, and I feel like it is completely my fault.

I'm the one who insisted on the no-sex rule, so for me to be the one to crack under the pressure of it—well, that's not exactly something I take pride in.

Except...it's Gabe.

Which means pretending like I'm not thinking about last week, about every week before that, is like pretending I don't notice when he walks around the apartment half-dressed and damp from the shower. Like pretending I don't still know exactly how he sounds when he—

I stab my chopsticks into the noodles a little harder than necessary.

He glances over, catching the motion out of the corner of his eye. "You okay over there?"

"Yeah," I say quickly. Too quickly. "Just trying to get a piece of broccoli."

He says nothing at first, just watches me for a second too long before going back to his sauce packets: one elbow resting on his knee, brow furrowed like the fate of dinner depends on picking the right one.

"Sage."

I look up.

"Do you want the sweet and sour or the chili garlic?"

"Why are you asking me like this is a hostage negotiation?"

"Because it is. There's only one of each."

I blink. "You're the one who ordered five different sauces."

"For variety," he says, deadpan. "But now I have regrets. I didn't expect to like all of them."

I snort, against my better judgment. "You're the most dramatic man alive."

He raises an eyebrow. "*I'm* dramatic?"

"You're literally staging a condiment crisis."

Gabe gives a lazy shrug, like he's unbothered. "I just have standards."

"Uh-huh. Sure. Next you'll be monologuing about egg-roll betrayal."

He smirks. "You say that like Liam wouldn't."

"He would. But at least he owns it. You act all chill, but deep down? Secret drama goblin."

"I'm offended."

"No, you're not."

And just like that, it's a little easier to breathe. I lean back into the couch, noodles forgotten, my legs stretched out just enough to nudge the coffee table.

We fall quiet again, but it's not the same kind of quiet.

He moves first—leans forward to grab something, but instead of going for his own carton, he reaches straight into mine. His shoulder grazes mine, just barely, and he plucks out an egg roll like he didn't just invade my personal space with the stealth of a cat.

"Hey!" I yelp, flailing my chopsticks in his direction as he leans back, smug, holding the egg roll just out of reach like a schoolyard bully with a crush.

"You had three already," he says, tilting his head. "I'm just enforcing fair distribution."

"I was saving that one."

"For what? Emotional support?"

"Exactly." I lunge for it half-heartedly, just enough to brush his wrist. "Give it back, Keaton."

He chuckles, low and real, and shifts like he might, only to pull it farther away at the last second.

"Oh, you asshole."

I launch forward before I think better of it, climbing over the couch cushions and reaching for his wrist. He jerks back in surprise, laughing as I clamber into his space, practically tackling him as we wrestle over a single egg roll as though our pride depends on it.

Because, obviously, it does.

"Give. It. Back," I huff, hands grappling for his, legs braced awkwardly on either side of his lap now.

"Too slow," he says, grinning up at me.

I pause. Just for a second.

Because somewhere in the middle of all the movement, I end up straddling him, one hand pressed to his chest, both of us breathing harder than the situation requires. His smile falters, just slightly, and my pulse thuds louder in my ears.

Neither of us moves.

My fingers are still curled around his wrist, but the fight's long gone. All I can feel is the heat of him beneath me—his chest rising against my palm, the shape of his thighs under mine, the quiet burn in his gaze that says he knows exactly what this looks like. What it feels like.

I should move. Say something, anything.

Instead, my breath catches.

And suddenly I'm thinking about how easy it would be to close the space between us. About how he tastes, how he sounds when I kiss him like I mean it. My body leans in the tiniest bit, betraying every rule I set like it was a suggestion, not a boundary.

His eyes flick down to my mouth.

Then he leans in, just barely, and murmurs, so close I feel it against my skin: "No sex, remember?"

Before I can even curse him for it, he shoves the egg roll in his mouth and chews with a smug, satisfied crunch.

I just stare at him.

For a solid, full-body beat, I don't move, I don't blink, I don't breathe.

He swallows and grins, mouth still half-full, eyes dancing with laughter. "Worth it," he mumbles around the bite.

I climb off him wordlessly, grab the nearest throw pillow, and launch it at his stupid, smug face.

It hits him square in the chest, but he's already laughing—head tipped back, full and obnoxious, like I didn't just come dangerously close to breaking my rule *again* because of one stolen egg roll.

I don't give him the satisfaction of a response. I just turn on my heel and head straight for my room, slamming the door behind me hard enough to rattle the frame.

I lean against it for a second, eyes closed, breath shaky.

And all I can see, feel, is the weight of him beneath me, the rasp of his voice against my mouth, the smirk he wore when he said it.

No sex, remember?

Goddammit.

I push off the door and head toward the bed, yanking my T-shirt over my head as I go.

I don't even bother turning the light on.

TEN

GABE

Morning light seeps through the blinds in soft, golden stripes, warming the tile under my feet and catching on the dust motes in the air like something out of a goddamn commercial.

For once, I actually slept.

Not well, exactly. Not deeply. But better than I have all week.

Because last night, after all the chaos and rule-breaking and nearly touching her again, she laughed.

Really laughed.

Let me see her smile without biting it back or hiding behind a smartass comment.

I'd forgotten what that looked like on her. It used to be all I wanted.

I'm halfway through making coffee, still riding that small, stupid high, when I hear the bathroom door creak open.

I don't think anything of it at first, just assume Sage is up, maybe heading back to her room or rummaging for clean clothes. It's quiet, the kind of morning where everything still feels slightly out of focus. The kind where you can almost trick yourself into thinking things are simple.

And then she walks straight past the kitchen entryway.

Naked.

Like, completely naked.

Not a towel, not a T-shirt, just dripping wet and moving like I'm not standing ten feet away with a coffee mug halfway to my mouth.

My eyes catch, before I can stop them, on the slope of her back, the water tracking down her spine, the quiet confidence in every step, like she does this every day, like it's not the single hottest thing I've ever seen.

And then she turns just enough for the light to hit—

Metal.

A glint across her chest, silver bars where my mouth used to be.

My throat goes dry.

I remember how it felt, how she felt, beneath me, breathing hard, fingers tangled in my hair while I took my time with each piercing. My tongue curled slowly around one, then the other, chasing that soft noise she only ever made when I—

I drag in a sharp breath and squeeze my eyes shut.

"This is fine," I mutter, mostly to myself.

Behind me, the fridge opens.

"What's fine?" she asks, all soft and sweet, like she didn't just walk through the kitchen like a damn fever dream.

I turn, slowly, because of course she heard me. Of course she's standing there now, facing me like nothing's out of the ordinary. One hip cocked, bottle of orange juice in her hand, not a single thread of clothing to her name.

"You're not wearing anything," I say, like it's news to either of us.

"We're in a heat wave," she says, lips pushing out in a mock pout that's anything but innocent.

She steps around me, close enough that I can smell her

shampoo—something citrusy, with a hint of jasmine—clinging to damp skin, and leans toward the cabinet overhead.

The bare line of her hip grazes my own, and her arm brushes mine.

And then she pauses, tilting her head like she's just remembered something. "Excuse me," she says softly, turning back toward the counter.

She doesn't wait for me to move. Just squeezes past again, and this time her chest presses against me—light, intentional, enough to short-circuit every working part of my brain.

I don't think. I just react.

One hand lands on the counter behind her, the other catches her hip. I pin her there, not rough, not even tight, just enough to hold her still. Enough to feel the sharp hitch in her breath, the way she looks up at me, eyes wide but not surprised.

Her lips part like she's going to say something. I dip my head without meaning to, forehead nearly brushing hers.

And then she lifts her arm, slow, effortless, and points to the fridge just beside us.

I don't look at first.

But I don't need to.

Her voice is calm, sweet, unforgiving.

"No sex, remember?"

My gaze shifts.

Cohabitation Bible
No sex with roommates

I drop my hands like I've been burned.

She slips past me again, this time with a smile in her voice. "Glad we're on the same page."

ELEVEN

SAGE

The bathroom at Wes and Savannah's is already too warm, the little box fan on the counter doing absolutely nothing against the lingering heat. The window's cracked, but it doesn't help much— just lets in the sounds of a lawn mower two yards over and the next-door neighbor's very vocal cockapoo.

Savannah's in a cropped tank and soft lounge shorts, her long red hair clipped up in a half-hearted twist that's slowly coming undone. She's dancing barefoot to the same pop remix that's been in the girls' group chat all week, singing into her foundation brush like a mic while I line my lips at the mirror beside her.

We're meeting Gen and Hannah at Harry's in an hour. Girls' night, minus the drinks for Savannah—because pregnant people, apparently, don't vibe with tequila.

We've done this whole pregame routine a hundred times. Loud music, shared mirror space, perfume clouding the air like fog. Usually we're laughing, already a little unhinged before we even leave the house.

Tonight, I'm quieter than usual.

Not enough for most people to notice.

But Savannah does.

She always does.

"You haven't judged a single song on this playlist," she says, glancing at me through the mirror. "And you haven't said you're going to make out with a stranger just to feel something. Which, let's be honest, is kind of your thing."

I smirk, but it barely makes it to one side of my face. "Maybe I'm evolving."

She twists the cap on her lip gloss and studies me like she's already figured it out. "Or maybe you're still thinking about Gabe."

My hand stills just long enough for her to know she's right.

I grab the sweating glass beside me and take a long gulp of the Tequila Sunrise Savannah insisted on making me.

"If I can't drink," she'd said earlier, one hand resting on her non-existent bump like it was her free pass for peer pressure, "you better drink enough for both of us."

So, I am.

Kind of.

Savannah watches me over the rim of her compact. "That's not an answer."

"It's tequila," I say, wiping my mouth. "It doesn't need an answer."

"Sage."

I sigh and set the glass down a little too hard on the counter. "I'm fine, Sav."

"You're not," she says gently. "You've been weird all week. And ever since you and Gabe made that 'no sex' deal—which, by the way, has got to be the dumbest agreement ever forged between two people who clearly want to crawl each other like jungle gyms—"

"Jesus." I laugh, half-choking on the rest of my drink. "Well, we already broke it once, so I doubt it's that."

Savannah stops mid-lip gloss swipe and turns her head slowly. "Excuse me?"

I wave a hand. "It was a one-time thing."

"A one-time—? Sage. Babe, that's not the kind of detail you just forget to mention."

"It wasn't a big deal."

Sav gives me the most deadpan stare imaginable. "You slept with Gabe, again, after making a No-Sex Pact. That is, in fact, the definition of a big deal."

I shrug, pretending I'm still interested in fixing my eyeliner. "The rule's still in effect."

She blinks. "Oh my God. You're reinstating the rule?"

"It's more of a...re-commitment," I mutter.

"To what? Emotional torture?"

I laugh despite myself, shaking my head. "I'd venture to call it physical torture as well."

Savannah snorts. "Yeah, no shit."

I don't say anything else, because the truth is, she's not wrong.

About any of it.

"I don't know, Sav." I twist the cap back onto my gloss and stare down at the counter like it might have answers. "It's weird. With me and Gabe. One day I'm thinking maybe it's worth bringing up— like, really bringing up. It's been months since him and Kara broke up, and it's been radio silence. No drama, no backslide. It actually seems like he's committed this time."

Savannah doesn't say anything. She doesn't have to.

"But it's complicated," I go on. "We're roommates. And...well. You were there."

That's all I say—all I *have* to say.

Her expression shifts, barely, but I see it. She remembers. The hotel. The reception.

"He hurt you," she says quietly. "More than once."

I nod. "And I let him."

"You trusted him."

"Yeah." My voice is soft. "And I don't know if I can do that again. Even if he is different now. Even if part of me still..." I stop.

Savannah reaches over and squeezes my hand. "You don't owe him anything," she says. "But you owe yourself the truth."

I grab my drink, take another long sip, and slip into the guest room, which, over time, has become my unspoken home-away-from-home in my brother's house.

The dress is already laid out on the bed. Strappy, low-backed, fitted in that subtle, dangerous way. The fabric's soft, moves with me, and the color—

Burnt orange.

Not the same one I wore to the rehearsal dinner, but close enough that it might register.

Not that I'm thinking about that.

I pull it on, adjusting the hem, smoothing it down over my hips like I'm not aware of exactly how it looks.

When I step back into the bathroom, Savannah looks up from her mascara and gives a soft, knowing "Damn."

I arch a brow. "Too much?"

She smirks. "Not even close."

I turn back to the mirror, adjusting my gold earrings as I drain the last of my drink.

Just a color. Just a dress.

That's all.

Besides, I don't even know if he's going to be there tonight.

Harry's is already packed by the time we get there.

That early summer kind of crowd—college kids clinging to their last few nights in town, locals pretending they don't care the bar's about to get quiet again. The energy's buzzy, a little reckless. Like everyone's trying to squeeze something in before it's too late.

It's loud, sticky, humid in that is-the-air-conditioning-broken-or-just-trying-its-best kind of way. The bass from the speakers rattles in my chest, the lights strobe too bright overhead, and someone bumps into me on the way through the door with a slurred apology and a half-spilled drink.

It smells like beer and cheap cologne and vanilla body spray—exactly like it always does. Exactly the way I like it.

Gen and Hannah are already perched at the bar when we walk in, half-finished drinks in front of them, leaning shoulder-to-shoulder and talking fast, as though they've just picked up the thread of a story they've been waiting all day to tell. They spot us instantly, waving us over.

Savannah beelines for an open stool and orders a ginger ale, while I slide onto the seat beside Hannah.

"Look who decided to show up," Hannah says, grinning as she throws her arm around my shoulders.

"Look who decided to rejoin society," I shoot back. "I was starting to think Liam had you locked in a tower."

"Please. I was willingly locked," she says, lifting her glass. "And to be fair, I did move in."

Gen grins. "Yeah, and you haven't come up for air since."

"I love a man with snacks and central air," Hannah says with a dramatic sigh.

We all laugh—because we get it.

"I missed this," she adds after a beat. "Missed you."

"I missed you more," I say, and mean it.

We clink glasses, hers fizzy and pink, mine amber and strong.

For a moment, that's all there is—us, the noise, the drinks, the familiar rhythm of a night that already feels like a memory before it's even really started.

We don't get to do this as much as we used to.

Somewhere between the third round and Gen trying to convince the bartender to play early-2000s throwbacks, we fully lose the plot.

There's glitter on my arms. I don't know where it came from.

Savannah's doubled over laughing at something Hannah said that definitely wasn't that funny, but it doesn't matter—we're all wheezing anyway.

I'm warm in that slow, humming kind of way. Not sloppy. Not out of control. Just...happy.

Hannah nudges me with her shoulder, eyes gleaming. "God, I needed this."

I nod, then squint at the bottles lining the back bar.

"No," she says immediately, catching the look on my face. "Sage. Don't you dare—"

But I'm already sliding off my stool, leaning way too far over the bar like I work here, and grabbing the first bottle of tequila my hand lands on.

The bartender is conveniently nowhere in sight.

"Sage—"

"Open up, Broadway." I grin, unscrewing the cap with a flourish. "This is payback for ditching me for domestic bliss."

Hannah barely gets her mouth open before I'm pouring, tequila sloshing into her mouth and partially down her throat as she splutters and laughs at the same time.

Gen lets out a dramatic gasp. "Oh my God, we're gonna get banned from drinking here again."

"We were never actually banned," I say, hopping down and recapping the bottle with all the grace of someone who should not be handling open liquor. "It was more of a stern talking-to."

Savannah raises her ginger ale in a toast. "To stern talking-tos."

"To bad decisions," Hannah adds, wiping her mouth.

I grin and clink my glass against hers. "To all the above."

I'm still laughing when I feel the shift.

A ripple behind me—like the energy in the room recalibrates without warning.

"Can I go next?" a low voice asks, smooth and smug and just the right amount of dirty.

We all turn at once.

Liam's leaning in behind Hannah, hand resting casually on the back of her stool, eyes locked on her like she's the only person in the building.

She blinks up at him, her face still flushed from tequila and laughter. "Go what?"

He lifts a brow. "Do whatever she just did to you."

"Oh my God," Gen mutters, half amused, half scandalized.

Hannah just shakes her head, grinning as she tugs him in for a kiss like it's the most natural thing in the world.

And, suddenly, I know.

If Liam's here, if they're here, then so is he.

I feel it before I see him. That static pull at the back of my neck, the quiet gravity that only ever means one thing.

I don't turn right away.

Instead, I reach for my drink, still half-full, still cold, and wrap my fingers around the glass like I've got all the time in the world. I lift the straw to my lips, slow and deliberate, and let my tongue flick against it just slightly before taking a sip.

The kind of move you don't think about when no one's watching—the kind you only make when you know someone is.

And I know he is.

"Nice dress."

The hairs on the back of my neck stand on end as I feel his breath ghost past my skin, low and close and entirely unfair.

I don't flinch, I don't turn.

I take another slow sip, letting my tongue drag slightly against the straw before I set the glass back down.

Then, finally, I glance over my shoulder.

"Eh," I say, lifting one shoulder in a lazy shrug. "This ol' thing?"

His eyes flick down, just briefly. "Hard to think straight when you look like that." There's a pause—tight, loaded. "I'm a little distracted."

My mouth curves, slow and dangerous. "That sounds like a you problem."

He huffs a quiet laugh.

But he doesn't move.

Doesn't look away.

And neither do I.

The moment stretches, tight and humming, until:

"Jesus Christ," Liam mutters as he walks past us. "Just fuck already."

I roll my eyes, but before I can say anything, Savannah, sweet, oblivious, glowing, starts to chime in.

"Oh, they al—"

My head snaps in her direction, and she catches the look before I even have to say it.

She shuts her mouth with a soft, polite sip of her ginger ale. "Right," she says lightly. "Never mind."

Gabe's still watching me, still standing close.

I take another slow sip of my drink.

Then someone yells for shots, and the moment breaks.

Just like that, the energy shifts, the spell snaps.

Music blares. Someone knocks over a glass. Gen's halfway into a debate with the bartender about what actually counts as top-shelf. Jackson's standing behind her with a hand on her lower back, watching the whole thing unfold like he's used to this exact brand of chaos.

Hannah disappears into the crowd, probably on her way to drag Liam away from whatever volume war he's about to start with the sound system. Wes is tucked in beside Savannah, one hand resting on her knee, the other keeping her ginger ale steady, like she might shatter if he lets her go.

And then the opening notes of "Africa" by Toto hit the speakers.

"Oh, *come on*," I hear Hannah groan somewhere behind me.

Liam's voice cuts above the noise, loud, proud, and way too into it, already shouting the lyrics like the whole bar is his personal karaoke stage.

"He's waited all night for this," Savannah says, shaking her head.

"I swear it's wired into his DNA," Gen mutters.

That's when I slip out the back.

The patio's mostly empty, everyone else drawn to the noise and nostalgia inside. The air's still warm, but quieter, the bass just a muted thump against the wall.

I lean against the railing, exhale slowly, and let myself breathe.

Then the door swings open.

I know it's him before I even look.

But I don't get the chance to turn, because a second later, I'm spun around and pinned against the brick, his hands braced on either side of my head, his body a heat I can feel everywhere, his green eyes now dark and unflinching.

"You have no idea what you're doing to me," Gabe says, voice low and wrecked.

I blink up at him slowly, tilt my head like I'm thinking.

Then I shrug.

"Maybe you're just easy."

He exhales hard through his nose, like he's trying not to lose it.

Like I want him to.

His gaze flicks over my face, sharp and heated. "Or maybe...*you miss me.*"

That hits harder than it should.

I keep my expression neutral. Bored, even.

"Don't flatter yourself."

He smirks, but there's no humor in it. He steps in closer. "Oh? Then why'd you wear that dress?"

I say nothing.

He leans in, voice low and rough. "Don't act like you didn't know I'd be here."

I lift my chin, unfazed. "It's my perfect shade. Complements my coloring."

That smirk returns, tight, hungry, dangerous.

His gaze drops for a fraction of a second before coming back to mine, darker now. Rougher.

"You know what else complements your coloring?" he murmurs. "Walking around *completely fucking naked* yesterday morning."

My breath catches—but I don't move.

He steps in closer, crowding me against the wall. "You really think I didn't notice the way the steam made your skin glow? The water sliding down your stomach, over those piercings, dripping off your hips like you were begging me to lose it?"

My pulse kicks. Still, I say nothing.

His eyes burn into mine. "I heard you, you know," he adds, voice nearly a whisper now. "Afterward. When you went to your room."

I blink, heart slamming into my breastbone.

"I could tell you were trying to be quiet. But I could hear it. Your moans." He leans in, lips not quite touching mine, breath hot. "The way you sounded when you touched yourself."

My whole body stills.

Then he keeps going—slow, deliberate, and cruel.

"Did being watched turn you on?" he murmurs. "Knowing I could hear you? I imagined you were soaked. I imagined sliding into that room, sinking to my knees, putting my mouth on you before you could tell me no."

My breath catches.

He doesn't stop.

"All you had to do was say my name," he whispers, "and I

would've been in there with my head between those perfect fucking thighs."

I blink up at him, my voice surprisingly steady. "Then why didn't you?"

He smirks. "I'm a gentleman."

I snort. It comes out dry. "*Hardly.*"

He inches closer, slow and deliberate, until his lips just barely graze mine.

Not a kiss, not yet, just heat and promise and the threat of it.

I tilt my chin, eyes locked on his.

"I did, you know," I murmur. "Say your name while I fingered myself. While I made myself come."

He stills.

"If you were really listening," I add, soft and wicked, "I would've thought you'd have heard it."

And that's all it takes.

His mouth crashes into mine, hungry and rough, like he's starved for it—like I've been torturing him, and maybe I have. Maybe that was the goal. His hands find my hips and grip tight, pulling me flush against him as his tongue slides against mine, hot and insistent. There's nothing soft about it. It's all teeth and need and months of everything we've been pretending not to feel.

My back hits the brick again, and he groans against my mouth as I fist the front of his shirt and drag him closer, like I could pull him under my skin if I tried hard enough.

One of his hands trails up my thigh, fingertips dragging over the hem of my dress, making me gasp into his mouth. He eats the sound like it's what he came out here for.

"You drive me fucking insane," he mutters against my jaw, lips trailing lower. "Do you know that?"

I don't answer.

I just yank him back in and kiss him like I mean it.

Because I do.

Even if I still don't know what the hell that means.

His hand slides up my thigh, slow and deliberate, fingers brushing against the inside like he's testing how far he can push.

Then he leans in, lips grazing the shell of my ear.

"If I reached under this dress," he murmurs, voice thick with want, "would I find you wet for me, baby?"

My breath catches, because he already knows the answer.

And I hate that he does.

I meet his eyes, defiant, breathless.

"I don't know," I say, voice low. "Why don't you find out?"

His gaze darkens, as though understanding I just handed him permission wrapped in a dare.

One hand slips under the hem of my dress, fingers trailing up—slow, reverent, filthy.

There's a beat where I think he might pause, might hesitate. He doesn't.

He groans when he realizes.

"No panties?" he murmurs, like it physically pains him to say it out loud.

I smirk. "Told you it was hot out."

His hand disappears beneath the hem of my dress, fingers grazing up my thigh—and then higher.

The second he finds me, he groans, low and wrecked.

"Fuck, Sage...you're soaked."

My breath catches. My whole body pulses toward him.

He leans in, voice rough in my ear. "You always get this wet for me?"

Then he swirls his fingers over my clit—once, twice—just enough to make my knees go soft, just enough for my hips to jerk forward on instinct.

"I should drop to my knees right now," he growls. "Taste you like this. Bet you'd be sweet—head tipped back, shaking, moaning my name all over again."

I press my palm against his chest, but I don't push him away.

Because, God help me, I want that too.

"You liked it yesterday," he says, voice low, lips brushing my jaw. "Liked knowing I saw you. Heard you. Bet it turned you on—thinking I might come in and catch you with your hand between your thighs."

I bite my lip hard enough to hurt.

His free hand skims down to grip my hip. "You're just as soaked now, and we're outside." His mouth ghosts across mine. "Someone could walk out here any second. Does that do it for you, baby? Knowing we could get caught?"

Of course, right then, the door creaks open behind him.

"I swear to God," Liam calls, his voice already laughing, "every time I play Toto, y'all disappear like horny teenagers."

Gabe doesn't move. Just keeps his body blocking mine completely, fingers still tucked between my thighs.

"Get a room!" Liam adds, already fading back inside.

I let out a slow, shaky breath. Of course it's Liam—fucking Liam.

Gabe's gaze finds mine again, heated and steady. "Want to?" He nods toward the parking lot. "Go home?"

I shake my head, though it takes everything I have to do it.

"Not tonight."

It hits like a bucket of cold water.

Which, on a night like this, sweat trickling down the back of my neck, should sound appealing.

But in the context of him? Of *this?*

It's just cold.

Sudden and sobering.

I feel myself start to crash out, the high of his hands on me, his mouth so close, spiraling into something messier. Something real.

Because it's never just physical with him, never has been.

With anyone else, I'm good at this part—at not caring, at pretending my chest doesn't tighten when it ends.

But Gabe?

Gabe's always been the exception. The one person I can't sleep with and walk away from unscathed.

And that's the part I can't afford to forget.

I can't get dropped like that again.

Not by him.

Not when I know how much it'll wreck me.

TWELVE

SAGE

I wake up with a headache that has nothing to do with alcohol.

It's the kind that sits behind your eyes, dull and persistent, like my body knows I'm not ready to deal with anything and is trying to slow me down until I am. I pull the covers over my head and will the world to give me just one more hour of pretending last night didn't happen.

Not the part where I poured tequila into Hannah's mouth straight from the bottle—that was actually relatively normal for a Friday night when she's in Atlanta—but the part where Gabe touched me like a map of my body was seared into his brain, and the part where he asked me if we could go home and finish what we started, and I almost said yes.

Almost.

I stay in bed until I smell maple sausage.

It sneaks under my door like a promise I didn't ask for, warm and familiar, the kind of smell that tugs at a memory before I can stop it.

Only it's not a memory, not really.

It's the shape of something I used to imagine, back when I still let myself believe there might be a version of us that made sense in the daylight. Sunday mornings with messy hair and shared coffee, him cooking breakfast while I sat on the counter and pretended not to watch the way his shirt clung to his back. A life that felt steady, maybe even safe.

But that version never existed, not outside the space between breakups.

We were never soft mornings and domestic rhythms; we were barely anything at all. Just moments, strung together with bad timing and worse decisions. A handful of nights when I convinced myself his hands on my body meant something more than habit.

Still, my stomach growls. Apparently, hunger doesn't care about emotional nuance.

I swing my legs out from under the blanket and grab the old, oversized T-shirt hanging off the bedpost—his, because of course it is—and pull it over my head before I can talk myself out of it. I peel off my bonnet and toss it onto the pillow, smoothing a hand over my hair like it matters.

The kitchen's quiet except for the low sizzle of the skillet and the hum of the fridge. He's barefoot, his back to me, moving like someone who doesn't realize I'm standing here wondering what the hell we're doing. Or maybe he does. Maybe he's just better at pretending this is normal.

He doesn't look up when I come in, doesn't make a joke or ask how I slept; he just shifts the pan slightly and forks another sausage onto a paper towel-lined plate.

He's not pushing, not talking, not even smiling, just making breakfast like it doesn't mean anything. Like it's not the closest we've ever come to being domestic, and it's happening after I shut him down at the bar and told him with my mouth what my body couldn't follow through on.

I sit on a stool and watch him for a second, my heart doing that stupid, stuttering thing it always does around him.

Because this doesn't mean anything, and that's always been the problem.

He finally glances over, eyes dropping to the shirt I'm wearing. His mouth tugs up at the corner—not a full smile, but something close.

"Son of a bitch," he says, turning back to the stove. "That's where my Falcons shirt went."

I look down like I haven't seen it before. "I left in it one morning. Last summer, I think."

He huffs a quiet laugh. "You've had it that long?"

"You weren't exactly asking me to come back for it."

He doesn't respond to that, just flips the last sausage onto a paper towel like I didn't say anything.

"I kept it," I add, softer now, "because it was the softest shirt I'd ever felt. It felt like a victimless crime."

"Yeah." He reaches for a plate, still not looking at me. "That's why I was pissed when I lost it."

That's it. No teasing, no flirtation, just a thread of something warm passed back and forth between us, the kind we don't know how to hold for long.

He sets the plate on the counter between us and grabs two forks from the drawer.

And just like that, we're sharing breakfast. In stolen clothes, talking about a night almost a year gone, like it might still matter.

I didn't keep the shirt because it was soft.

I mean...it *is* soft. But that's not why I kept it.

I kept it because I wanted something of his that wasn't temporary. Something that didn't come with strings or stipulations or Kara-shaped expiration dates. I wanted proof that, for one night, I mattered enough to be missed—that when he rolled over and realized I was gone, he noticed.

He didn't call, of course he didn't. And I told myself I didn't care. I folded the shirt, stuck it in the bottom of a drawer, and didn't wear it again for months.

But I never got rid of it, either.

Because some part of me was still waiting to be the exception, the one time he didn't go back to her.

And now here we are. Sharing breakfast as though that history isn't still humming under the surface. As though I didn't spend the better part of last year trying to forget the exact way he's standing right now. Barefoot, shoulders relaxed, like he's good at mornings.

Like we've ever had one like this before.

He slides the plate a little closer to me and hands over a fork. I take it without speaking, twirl it between my fingers like I'm trying to work up the nerve to use it.

He breaks the silence first.

"You still like the maple ones, right?"

I nod, and he spears one, sets it on my side of the plate like a peace offering.

I should say thank you, should smile or make a joke, pretend this is no big deal, but my throat's tight and my chest feels full and hollow all at once, so I just eat it instead.

He doesn't comment, just grabs one for himself and leans his hip against the counter like we do this all the time.

We eat like that for a while: quiet, slow, like neither of us knows what to do with the space we've made.

Because this wasn't who we were, not even close, but maybe, if I'm honest with myself, it was who I wanted us to be, just once.

He catches me watching him and lifts a brow. "What?"

I shake my head. "Nothing."

I think we both know that's a lie.

We continue to eat in silence. Not the strained kind. Just... quiet, like neither of us wants to be the first to break whatever this is.

I'm halfway through the second sausage when a memory

sneaks up on me—sharp and vivid, like the kind that's been waiting for the right moment to resurface.

"Do you remember that night we ended up at that shitty twenty-four-hour diner off Piedmont?" I ask, twirling the fork between my fingers.

Gabe looks over, brow furrowed. "Which time?"

"The one where everyone bailed after the bar," I say. "Jackson went home with Gen—pretty sure that was the first weekend after Gen finally admitted her feelings for him. Wes and Savannah were making out against her car like they forgot the rest of us existed. And Hannah—God." I laugh under my breath. "She was in town visiting and got so drunk she couldn't walk."

Gabe starts to grin, the memory clicking into place. "Right. Liam threw her over his shoulder like a fireman."

"She screamed at him the whole time," I say, grinning. "Called him a misogynist. Bit him on the shoulder."

"And then asked for mozzarella sticks," he adds, shaking his head.

I snort. "She was wearing those glitter heels that broke before we even got out of the Uber."

"And she made you take them off for her."

"Because I still had feeling in my fingers," I say, like that excuses it. "You gave her your socks."

"Which she left in the booth."

We both laugh, and for a moment it feels easy again. Familiar in a way that doesn't ache.

I remember watching them that night—Liam rolling his eyes while carrying Hannah, ignoring how she clawed at his back, like she didn't terrify him and delight him in equal measure. He didn't even like her back then, but he still would've fought anyone who looked at her wrong. That kind of care was instinctive.

I thought maybe, if I waited long enough, Gabe would care about me like that.

I glance over at him now—still barefoot, still quiet, still here.

I think part of me is still waiting.

We fall quiet again, the silence expectant. Not tense, not uncomfortable—just full.

I twirl my fork once, twice, then set it down and look at my plate instead of him. "I loved you, you know. Back then."

The words come out lighter than they feel, like I'm trying to pass them off as something casual. But they hang there, suspended in the space between us.

Gabe doesn't answer right away. I hear the soft clink of his fork against the plate as he sets it aside, slow and deliberate.

"Yeah," he says. "I think I knew."

And maybe he did, or maybe he just knows now, with the benefit of hindsight and all the damage done.

I keep my gaze averted as I add, "It's not...like that anymore."

A lie. But one I've gotten good at telling.

He doesn't call me on it. Just nods, then says, quietly—

"I'm sorry. For back then...and for a few months ago...and all the time in between."

That part almost undoes me.

Because it's not just an apology for the ghost of a relationship we never had; it's for the way he kept showing up and leaving like it didn't cost me something every single time.

I don't say anything. I just nod, because I can't trust my voice, and we both know it.

We finish eating in silence, forks scraping gently against the plates. The air between us stills, not heavy, just...different. Something has shifted, something has cracked.

And maybe it's not everything, but it's more than I ever thought I'd get.

THIRTEEN

GABE

It's been forty-five days since Sage sat across from me at the kitchen counter in my T-shirt, picked at her breakfast like it might say too much, and told me she loved me—back then.

She said it like it was a throwaway, like she wasn't still wearing the shirt a year after she left in it.

But the past tense clung to every syllable.

Back then.

Not *now.*

I haven't been able to stop hearing it since.

We haven't hooked up again, not since the bar, when she kissed me back like she meant it, pulled me close like she was starving for it—until Liam walked out, and she stepped away as though she'd been caught stealing something that didn't belong to her.

She doesn't talk about that night, and doesn't talk about the morning after, either.

But we've found something else in the quiet.

She still drinks my coffee, still hogs the blanket, still hums when she's folding laundry like she doesn't realize I can hear her from the other room.

We're in a rhythm. Comfortable, predictable, and I've been afraid to touch it, because if back then was her way of drawing a line, I don't know what happens if I try to cross it.

Right now, she's in the kitchen, barefoot and singing off-key to some playlist that can't decide between soulful and poppy. Her hair's a mess, her tank top's slipping off one shoulder.

I'm supposed to be chopping onions, but all I can do is watch her.

She catches me staring and arches a brow. "You're about to lose a thumb."

"Occupational hazard," I mutter, setting the knife down as she slides in to take over.

"You're hopeless," she says, but it's warm. Teasing, like she doesn't mind being seen.

She's close enough that I can smell her shampoo, feel the heat coming off her skin.

She leans forward to scrape the onions into the pan, her shoulder brushing mine. She doesn't flinch. Doesn't move away.

The sizzle picks up as she adds garlic, tossing it all with the flick of her wrist like she's done it a hundred times before.

And then, as casually as if she's commenting on the weather, she says, "You should kiss me."

I freeze. "What?"

She doesn't look at me, doesn't repeat herself. Just keeps stirring, unbothered, like she didn't just knock the wind out of me.

I must've misheard her, or maybe she's joking—some offhand, throwaway thing meant to disarm me like usual. Except her tone wasn't teasing. It was soft, steady, like she meant it.

But she's still cooking, still calm. If she meant it, wouldn't she... do something? Look at me? Smile?

Maybe it's a test, or maybe I'm imagining it because I want it to be real. Maybe I've finally lost it.

"Did you..." I clear my throat. "Did you just say I should kiss you?"

She shrugs, still not looking at me. "Yeah."

Just *yeah*. Like we're talking about what time the groceries are being delivered.

My pulse is in my ears now. I can't read her—I've never been able to, not really. But this? This is different. She doesn't say things like this; she doesn't ask. She walks away, she shuts down.

But she's not walking away now. She's not pulling back.

She's just...waiting.

Still stirring, still calm.

And I'm standing here trying to remember how to breathe.

She shrugs and repeats herself. "Yeah."

Just that. No buildup, no punchline.

And I stand there like an idiot. Frozen, because I want to— God, I want to. But I don't know if I'm allowed to. If this is real, or if she's going to regret it the second my hands are on her.

The silence stretches a little too long.

She scoffs under her breath, still not facing me. "Man, you really make a girl feel desired, don't you?"

That hits harder than it should.

Before I can say anything, she adds, "Forget it. It was a dumb idea."

Her voice cracks on the word *dumb*, barely audible over the sizzle in the pan, but I hear it. And suddenly it's not a joke anymore, not really.

She's pulling away again, and I'm letting her, because I'm afraid of being wrong. Of pushing too hard, of ruining whatever this is. But maybe not doing anything is ruining it, too.

"Sage."

She doesn't look at me.

I step closer. "Sage," I say again, softer this time. "It wasn't a dumb idea."

That gets her. She turns, slowly, guarded but curious. Her eyes meet mine, wary, like she's bracing for impact.

"I just didn't want to screw it up," I say. "But if you meant it—if this is something you want..."

I trail off, because I'm not sure how to finish that sentence without handing her every part of me I've been holding back.

She studies me for a long second, like she's trying to decide if it's safe to trust this—to trust me.

Then, barely above a whisper:

"I did mean it."

The room goes still.

She's looking at me like she's daring me to call her bluff. Like she won't say it again if I don't move now.

But I don't rush.

I just watch her. Let myself look, really look, at the way her mouth curves with uncertainty, the way her breath catches when I don't immediately close the distance. And for once, I don't let the moment scare me off.

I step in.

Close enough to feel her breath mix with mine.

Close enough to see the freckles she hates and the softness in her eyes she tries to cover with sarcasm.

We just stand there, barely touching, like we're both waiting for the other to make the final move.

And then I do.

I kiss her.

Not like I did outside the bar. Not like all the other times, where it was heat and history and too many tangled nights trying to pretend we didn't feel anything deeper than lust.

This is slower, still.

Her lips part like a sigh against mine, and I cup her jaw gently, like I'm afraid she'll vanish if I touch her too hard.

We stay like that for a long time, just kissing, like we've got nowhere else to be, like it's the only language we know.

She presses closer, hands curling in the front of my shirt, and I can feel her heart pounding against my chest. Fast. Unsteady. Just like mine.

When she breaks the kiss to breathe, she doesn't step back.

Neither do I.

I lean over to gently shut off the burner on the stove before turning my attention to her.

I kiss her again, deeper this time, but still slow, still careful. And when her hand slides up the back of my neck, anchoring herself there, something breaks open in me.

I pull her into me fully, lift her gently off the floor, and she wraps her legs around my waist like it's the most natural thing in the world.

She doesn't say anything, doesn't ask where we're going.

She knows.

I carry her down the hall, her mouth warm against my throat, her fingers fisting in my shirt as if she's afraid I'll change my mind.

But I won't.

Not this time.

The door creaks open with the touch of my foot, and I don't bother with the light. The room glows dimly from the hallway behind us, just enough to see the outline of her face as I move toward the bed.

I lower her onto the mattress slowly, like she's something fragile. Like this matters.

Because it does.

She looks up at me, wide-eyed, her braids spilling across my pillow, streaked through with strands of blue. The color catches in the soft light, and for a second, I forget how to breathe.

She used to do that when we first met—play with color, always trying something new with her appearance, with the way she took up space. Her style changed with her moods; her hair always included some shade of vibrant—burgundy, teal, gold, loud and beautiful and hers.

But somewhere along the way, that color drained. I don't know if it was life, or hurt, or me. Probably some mix of all three. Her edges got quieter, her light pulled inward. The creativity that used to radiate from her dulled like she didn't see the point anymore.

But now—

Now the blue is back, woven through like a quiet declaration.

And I can't stop looking at her.

She doesn't say anything.

She doesn't have to.

I settle beside her and kiss her again—softer than before, slower, like I'm learning her all over again.

And she lets me.

Her hands come up to frame my face, thumbs brushing along my jaw. Her mouth parts against mine and I swear it feels like forgiveness, like relief, like something we've both been aching toward without knowing how to ask for it.

When I slide my hand beneath her tank top, she breathes out like she's been holding it in for years. I don't rush. I don't fumble. I just touch her—slow, reverent, like she's something I'm choosing this time. Not falling into. Not escaping with. *Choosing.*

She sits up just enough to pull her shirt over her head, and I follow her lead, peeling off mine and letting it fall to the floor.

Our eyes lock.

This is not how it's ever been, not between us, not like this.

Because this isn't just sex.

It's not about release or nostalgia or the high of pretending we don't care.

This is something else, something that feels terrifying in its simplicity.

And I think we both know it.

She reaches for the clasp of her bra, pauses like she's waiting to see if I'll look away.

I don't. Not because I'm trying to prove something, but because this moment feels sacred. Because I want her to see I mean it—that I'm here, really here, and I'm not going anywhere.

The bra slips from her shoulders. I trace a hand over the curve of her waist, let it settle just above the hem of her shorts. She leans into the touch like she's been waiting for it, like maybe she's finally done pretending this doesn't matter.

I kiss her again, slower this time, more deliberate. She tastes like toothpaste and tea and something warmer, something that feels like home.

She hooks her fingers into the waistband of her shorts and nudges them down her hips. I follow, my hands brushing over her thighs as I help ease them off, every inch of her revealed like a truth I don't deserve but get to hold anyway.

There's no rush, no fumbling, just the sound of our breathing, the rustle of sheets, and the quiet pull of gravity between us.

When I move to undress, she stops me with a touch to my chest —gentle, open-palmed, not asking me to wait, just to see her, to be here, fully.

And I am.

God, I am.

I ease her back into the pillows and settle beside her, close enough that our foreheads touch. Her eyes search mine, and whatever she finds there, whatever she's been looking for, makes her smile, soft and sure.

She pulls me in again, and this time when we kiss, it's slower still. Like we're not kissing to start anything, but to stay right here in the feeling of it.

She shifts next to me, legs parting slightly, her thigh brushing against mine, and it hits me all over again—this is Sage. *Sage.* And she's here, with me, letting herself be seen, touched, loved.

I slide my hand down her side, over the curve of her hip, and lower it between her thighs. She's already wet, warm and open, and when I drag two fingers through her, she exhales sharply and arches into my palm.

Fuck.

I stroke her slowly, just enough to draw a shiver, to make her hips roll without thinking. Her breath hitches again when I circle her clit, featherlight at first, then firmer, more intentional. She grips my bicep, nails digging in, her forehead tipping forward to press against mine.

"Gabe," she whispers, the sound raw and pleading, like she's too full of feeling to hold it in.

I kiss her again, deep and slow, while I keep touching her, fingers sliding through her arousal, learning every response. When I slip one inside, her whole body tenses, then softens around me.

She's so fucking beautiful like this.

Open, unrushed, letting me in.

When I add a second finger, she moans, quiet, choked off by another kiss, and grinds down to meet the rhythm I've set.

She's not performing, she's not hiding, she's just feeling, and fuck if I'm not already half gone for it.

I pull back just enough to see her face, flushed and soft, her full lips parted, breath unsteady.

"I need you," she says, voice barely a breath. "Please."

I press my forehead to hers and whisper, "I've got you."

I move over her, between her legs, and she guides me with a hand around the back of my neck, pulling me down as though she can't bear the space between us anymore.

When I press into her, it's slow, careful, every inch a surrender. She gasps beneath me, legs wrapping around my waist, and I pause once I'm fully inside, both of us breathless from the way it means something this time.

We stay like that for a beat, breathing, pressed together, feeling it.

Then she rocks her hips gently, and we fall into a rhythm, slow and steady at first, like we're relearning what it means to be with each other. Like we're memorizing this, in case it's the only time we get it right.

Her hands roam my back, nails dragging lightly down my spine, and every movement is a question I already know the answer to.

I kiss her again as I thrust deeper, and she moans into my mouth—low and desperate and real.

This isn't about undoing each other. It's about holding each other together.

Her legs tighten around me, her body pulsing with every slow roll of my hips, and I feel her starting to come apart.

She breaks the kiss to whisper, "Don't stop."

I won't.

I couldn't, even if I tried.

Her body tightens around me as I push in deeper, and I force myself to keep my eyes open, to watch her.

She's looking back at me, wide-eyed, lips parted, like she can't quite believe this is happening either. Like she's just as undone by the softness of it as I am.

I bottom out slowly, carefully, and we both freeze—not because we're unsure, but because it's too much to rush.

Her eyes stay locked on mine.

And I swear, it knocks the breath out of me.

Because this is the part I never got. This part right here, being inside her like this, and seeing her see me. Not just the body, not just the heat, but me.

She's not looking away.

She's not hiding behind banter or distance or denial.

And I'm not hiding either.

There's no mask here, no push-pull game, just her, open and

real beneath me. And me, trying not to fall apart because she's letting me love her like this.

When I start to move again with slow, deliberate thrusts, her eyes flutter, but they stay on me. Her breath stutters every time I sink in, her fingers clenching around my shoulders like she needs the grounding.

I kiss her again, slow and messy and full of feeling, and when I pull back, she's still watching me like I'm the only thing keeping her tethered.

This is different; this is sacred. I've touched her before, but I've never had her like this, not fully, not when she's soft and open and meeting me right in the middle.

She lifts her hips to meet every stroke, her moans slipping out quieter now, meant just for me. The sound of her so honest, so unguarded, wraps around my ribs like a fist.

If I didn't already love her, this would've done it.

She tightens around me suddenly, a sharp gasp catching in her throat, and her eyes go glassy, like she's on the edge of falling apart.

"You're okay," I whisper, brushing a kiss over her cheekbone. "I've got you."

Her hand grabs mine, lacing our fingers together, pressing our joined palms into the bed beside her head, like she's trying to keep us anchored there.

I've never felt anything like this, never wanted anything this badly. Not sex, not closeness—*her*. I want her to know this isn't just desire. It's me, choosing her back.

She shudders, hips jerking beneath me, and I feel it, that moment when her whole body tightens, then trembles, and she comes with a breathless cry against my neck.

She clings to me like the world's slipping sideways.

And I hold her like it's not going anywhere.

She comes with her face tucked into my neck, her body pulsing around me, and it nearly undoes me on the spot.

Her breath stutters against my skin, fingers digging into my shoulders as if she needs to hold on or she'll float away.

I don't move right away; I just stay buried inside her, forehead pressed to hers, our chests rising and falling like we're trying to breathe each other back into place.

She let me see her, let me feel her like this. And it's not about the sex—not really. It's about the trust in her hands, in her eyes, in the way she held me like I was something worth reaching for.

I kiss her again, messy and uncoordinated, partly from how close I am to falling apart.

She's still trembling when I start to move again, slow and careful, chasing that last bit of friction. Her legs stay wrapped around my waist, holding me close, like she doesn't want me to leave even when it's over.

The pressure builds fast...too fast.

There's no distance this time, no detachment.

Just her, warm and soft and wrapped around me as though I've finally earned my place here.

My rhythm falters, and she notices, whispers my name again, quiet and certain, like permission.

That's all it takes.

I thrust deep one last time and groan into her mouth as I come, everything unraveling at once—months of restraint, years of wanting, all spilling out in the space between her arms.

She holds me through it, hands gentle in my hair, lips brushing the corner of my mouth.

It feels like a letting-go. But also, somehow, like a beginning.

I press a kiss to her collarbone, then another to the spot just below her jaw.

We stay like that, tangled together, our skin damp and our breaths syncing slowly into something steady.

Neither of us speaks; we don't have to, because for the first time in a long time, silence feels like safety.

She doesn't let go right away, and neither do I.

Her arms are still looped loosely around my neck, legs tangled with mine, and I keep my forehead pressed to hers, breathing her in, trying to memorize the shape of this quiet.

Eventually, she exhales a long, shaky breath and eases back, just enough to meet my eyes.

I reach up to brush one of her braids off her cheek, fingers skimming the soft curve of her face. "You okay?"

She nods.

"Really okay?" I ask, softer now. "Not the version you give everybody else."

That makes her smile, barely there, but real. "Yeah," she says. "I'm good. A little wrecked, but...good."

"Wrecked in a good way?"

Her laugh is quiet, breathy. "Yeah. In a good way."

I press a kiss to her temple and ease out of her slowly, gently, careful not to break whatever this is we've built between us. She flinches a little from the sensitivity and I rest a hand on her thigh, grounding her.

"I'll be right back," I say.

In the bathroom, I grab a warm towel, a bottle of water, one of my softest shirts from the drawer. When I come back, she's still in my bed, on my side now, half-curled beneath the covers like she belongs there.

We've shared a bed before—after parties, long nights, one too many drinks. Usually with a few feet of space between us. Sometimes after a hookup, when neither of us wanted to say goodbye yet but weren't brave enough to say why. Always quiet, always temporary.

I clean her up slowly, wiping between her thighs with as much care as I can. She watches me the whole time, eyes soft, saying nothing, but she doesn't look away.

Once I'm done, I toss the towel aside and hold out the shirt.

She takes it and pulls it on without a word. It swallows her, hangs loose over her thighs, short sleeves down to her elbows. Seeing her in it does something to my chest.

She settles back into the pillows, and I climb in beside her, pulling the blanket over both of us. She immediately shifts closer, pressing her cheek to my chest, her palm spreading over my ribs.

She's never done that before, either.

I keep one hand on her back, fingers tracing slow circles over her spine, the other resting gently over hers.

Her voice is barely above a whisper when she says, "This feels different."

I don't ask what she means.

Because I know.

"Yeah," I murmur. "It is."

We lie there for a long time, nothing but the sound of our breathing and the faint creak of the house settling around us.

And for the first time, she doesn't get up.

She doesn't put the walls back up.

She stays.

FOURTEEN

SAGE

It's been a week since I slept in Gabe's bed. Since he touched me like I was something precious and kissed me like he meant it.

Since then, everything's felt quieter. More careful.

We didn't talk about it afterward—not the next morning, not any of the mornings after. I went back to my room and he stayed in his. And even though we're still...whatever we are, the silence between us keeps shifting shape.

We haven't hooked up again, haven't even really kissed, but he makes me coffee in the morning, puts a hand on the small of my back when he brushes past me in the kitchen. Leaves the light on in the hallway if I come home late.

It's like we're playing house with our mouths sewn shut.

And I don't know what we are; I don't know what I'm allowed to ask for. But I know that every time he closes his bedroom door behind him at night, something inside me flinches.

At work, I try to keep busy. Stick to the routine, wipe the same part of the bar twice, overfill the lemons just to give my hands something to do.

But today, Harry calls me into the back office. Doesn't look up when I walk in, just keeps flipping through a folder on his desk like it's any other day.

"The deal's about to close," he says. "Bar's changing hands end of the month."

Just like that.

No soft lead-in, no warning.

I blink. "You're serious?"

He nods, still not looking at me. "Got the final paperwork yesterday. Pretty soon there will be a pretty new sign out front."

"And you're okay with it?"

He hesitates. "I thought I would be."

There's a pause, a long one.

"I feel...old," he adds, eyes still fixed on the paper in front of him. "Like maybe this place isn't mine anymore, even before I hand over the keys."

That's what breaks me.

Not the news, not the timeline.

Hearing him say that.

Because Harry's not that old—he's just tired, and maybe I am too. Or maybe I'm just scared that I've run out of places where I make sense.

I don't want something new; I want *this*. I want to fight for the thing I already built, even if it never had my name on the building.

I tell him I have a headache and need to leave early. Since I almost never call in sick or leave early, he lets me go without question.

I walk home in a fog and find Gabe in the kitchen when I get there—barefoot, moving around like he's trying not to make noise. There are vegetables on the cutting board and garlic on his fingers, and it smells like comfort, but I can't feel it.

He looks up as I drop my keys into the bowl by the door.

"You okay?" he asks, already reaching for the second glass of wine on the counter.

I shake my head. "Harry's selling the bar. Like, officially. He has the paperwork and everything."

An exhausted sigh escapes my lungs as I plop down at the kitchen table, my eyes locked on the far wall. The wine sits untouched in front of me.

Gabe moves a little slower after that, quieter. He turns down the burner, sets the knife aside, wipes his hands on a dish towel, and walks over to sit across from me.

"When's it happening?" he asks, voice low.

"End of the month." I laugh, but it's humorless. "Guess I should've seen it coming, but I didn't. I thought he'd drag his feet."

He nods, but doesn't say "I'm sorry" or "That sucks," just lets me talk. That's the thing about Gabe—sometimes he pushes too hard, but sometimes he knows exactly when not to say anything.

I wrap both hands around the wine glass, but I still don't take a sip. "He looked...sad," I say. "Like he wasn't sure if he was doing the right thing, but he'd already said yes, so he couldn't stop now."

Gabe's brow furrows. "You think he regrets it?"

"I don't know." I swallow. "I think it's hitting him how much of himself is in that place, and now he has to walk away from it."

I don't say it, but I feel that too. Like I'm about to lose the only thing that's ever made me feel steady. Like I'm watching my safety net burn and trying not to show that it hurts.

We sit in silence for a beat, the kind that doesn't need to be filled.

Then, soft: "What are you gonna do?"

I shrug. "Keep showing up until they lock me out, I guess."

He leans back in his chair, rubbing his palm across the back of his neck. "I'm sure they'll keep the staff."

I let out a breath through my nose, not quite a laugh. "Yeah. Maybe."

"But?" he prompts.

I take a sip of the wine, finally, and then set the glass back down a little too hard. "But it won't be the same. It's going corporate. Menu changes. Dress code. Branded napkins and bullshit slogans taped to the mirror in the bathroom."

He doesn't say anything, so I keep going, the words tumbling out now.

"Harry let it be what it was, ya know? Loud. Messy. Weird. It had soul. And once a chain takes over, that goes away. I don't want to work somewhere that treats it like a product instead of a place."

He nods slowly, but I can already see the wheels turning behind his eyes. I know that look.

The quiet calculation. The trying-to-solve-it look.

I should stop him. I should change the subject or leave the room.

But I don't.

He glances toward me again, cautious now. "You could buy it."

"Don't start that shit again, please."

It comes out sharper than I mean it to, but I don't walk it back. I can't.

He doesn't respond right away, but I can feel his eyes on me. I take another sip of wine, mostly just to have something to do with my hands.

He doesn't know what he's asking. Or maybe he does, and he just doesn't understand what it would cost me.

There's money, of course. I almost never talk about it, not even with Wes. A trust fund, set aside when my mom died—part of a life that never really felt like mine. Wes has one too, but he's always known what to do with it. He's always had direction, stability, plans.

Me? I was the one working odd shifts at three different bars in a year. Bouncing between cities. Picking up temp work, then ditching it because something shinier caught my eye. I made it look carefree on purpose.

Gabe saw it all back then too, and he never seemed to judge me for it. He used to call me free-spirited, said I wasn't motivated by capitalism like everyone else, like it was a choice. Like I had a philosophy.

Maybe I did, I don't know anymore.

Truth is, I didn't think I had what it took to stay anywhere long enough to build something. I was scared shitless of committing to anything I could break.

The trust fund? It's a trapdoor. A safety net I'm too afraid to step onto, because if I use it and fail, that's it. I'll have no one to blame but myself. No excuse, no fallback, just me and the proof I was never built to carry something real.

I set the wine glass down harder than I mean to. "You think I haven't thought about that?" I ask. "You think it hasn't been in the back of my mind since the second Harry told me?"

Gabe's expression shifts—careful now. "I didn't mean to push. I just...I think you'd be good at it."

"You *think*," I repeat, the words bitter on my tongue. "Everyone *thinks* I'd be good at something until I actually try."

"Sage—"

"No. You don't get it." My voice is rising now, shaking, but I don't stop. I can't stop. "You see me as this laid-back, don't-give-a-shit bartender with weird earrings and no plan, and you think it's charming. You think it's a choice, that I'm just too cool to care about owning anything."

I push away from the table and start pacing, hands in my hair, like if I keep moving I can outrun the panic pressing against my ribs. "You know why I never stay anywhere? Why I've never committed to anything longer than a playlist? Because deep down I don't think I can. Because I'm the one in the family who bails, who forgets birthdays, who disappears for music festivals and comes back with my scalp burnt and no money and another story about why I left the job I swore I liked."

He stays seated, watching me carefully, but I see the way his fingers flex against the table. He wants to say something, and maybe he should, but I keep going.

"I didn't choose to be a flighty mess. I became one because it was the only thing people ever expected from me. And now you want me to, what—use my mom's trust fund to buy a bar? To tie her name to something I'm statistically probably going to fail at?"

I laugh, and it's ugly. Harsh, too close to crying.

"You think I could handle that? Losing the last thing I have from her because I wanted to play pretend as a small business owner?"

My throat burns. My chest aches. But I'm too far in now to stop.

We don't talk about my mom. I seldom do in general—not because I don't think about her, but because I was so young when she passed that I don't even have a memory of her. Just stories, a handful of old photos, and a trust fund with her name on it, like a reminder I didn't earn.

I know Gabe knows; Wes has told him things over the last few years. I've seen it in the way he looks at me sometimes, usually around Mother's Day—like he's carrying pieces of grief I never got the chance to claim.

And maybe I do the same for him. I never ask, but I know enough to understand his grief is messier—sharper at the edges. His mother didn't leave him by dying. She left him while still breathing.

"I told you I can't, Gabe. Not because I don't want to. Because I don't believe I'd survive the fallout if I tried and it wasn't enough."

There's a long silence.

Then, quietly, "That's not what I was saying."

I finally look at him.

He's still seated, elbows on the table, hands open like he doesn't want to spook me.

"I wasn't pushing you," he says gently. "I wasn't trying to tell you what to do. I just—" He exhales, rubs a hand across his mouth.

"I just wanted you to remember you have options. That you're more capable than you think."

His voice is soft—not defensive, not combative, just steady. Like he's offering me something to hold onto instead of throwing something in my face.

But my body doesn't know what to do with kindness when I'm spiraling. It always reads like pity, like disappointment dressed up in concern.

"You think I'm capable," I say, the words brittle. "But that's the problem, Gabe. You don't know me. Not really."

He shifts like he's about to say something, but I don't let him. I can't. The words keep coming, too fast to stop.

"You think just because you've fucked me on and off for the last couple years, that means you know me?" I let out a dry laugh, sharp and humorless. "Come on, Gabe. Be serious. Half the time it was when you were bored, or lonely, or, God, for whatever reason Kara wasn't answering your calls that week."

His jaw tenses, but I'm already spiraling.

"I was the stand-in. The one you crawled back to when it was convenient, when it didn't work out with her. And I let you; I let you use me like a—like a fucking pit stop between breakdowns. Because I was too dumb, or too desperate, or whatever it was, to walk away."

My voice breaks, and I hate it. Hate the way it makes me sound small. But it's the truth, the messy, bleeding truth I've never said out loud.

"I wasn't a person to you," I finish, quieter now. "Not really, just something soft to land on until you went back to the life you actually wanted."

He stares at me.

No denial, no rebuttal.

Just...silence.

His shoulders rise with a slow breath—controlled, careful.

"I deserved some of that," he says finally, voice low. "Probably most of it."

He doesn't raise his voice, doesn't flinch. Just takes it in like a man used to standing in the middle of someone else's storm.

"But not all of it."

I cross my arms tightly over my chest, like I can hold myself together if I just squeeze hard enough.

He takes a step back—not away from me, not quite, but like he's putting space between us before he says something he can't unsay. "I haven't talked to Kara in months, not since I moved in here," he says quietly. "I left that part of my life behind for a reason. And yeah, I fucked up with you. I know I did, I know I kept coming back, and I never gave you the clarity you deserved. But this version of me, the one standing here now, he's not crawling back. He's here, and he's been here."

I look away, jaw clenched.

He waits a beat, giving me a chance to say something, anything.

But I don't.

"I don't even know why I'm here if you won't talk to me," he says. "If you won't let me be here."

His words are calm, not cruel. But they still knock the wind out of me.

"Then leave!" I snap, voice louder than I intend.

It echoes through the kitchen like something thrown.

We both freeze.

The words hang between us like smoke—acrid, impossible to take back.

The silence that follows is thick and suffocating.

He doesn't move, doesn't blink, just looks at me with something tired in his eyes, like he's sifting through all the versions of me he's known, trying to understand the one standing in front of him now.

My chest tightens. I want to say I didn't mean it, but the words stay lodged in my throat, stuck behind pride and panic and too many years of not saying the right thing at the right time.

He nods, slow, hollow. "Okay," he says at last, barely louder than a whisper.

Then he turns, grabs his keys from the hook by the door, and walks out.

The door clicks shut behind him, and I just stand there.

Frozen.

Waiting for the echo to fade.

I don't cry, not yet, not even when the silence starts to throb in my ears like a warning.

He'll come back; he has to.

His shoes are still by the door. His hoodie's on the back of the couch. He left his charger plugged in, his jacket slung over the dining chair. People don't leave for good without their stuff, and all of his stuff is here.

This is just a fight. A bad one, yeah, but we've had worse. Haven't we?

Except we haven't.

I drag in a shaky breath and sink into one of the kitchen chairs, the one he was just sitting in. It's still warm.

He didn't yell.

He didn't argue.

He just...left, which might be worse, honestly.

My fingers toy with the stem of my wine glass, still half-full, but my desire for it is long gone. I glance at the clock, as if I'll find something useful in the passage of minutes, a sign that he's on his way back.

He just needs space.

He'll come back.

He always does.

But even as I think it, something deep in my gut curls tight— because this time, for the first time, I'm not so sure.

FIFTEEN

SAGE

I don't sleep.

I lie in bed, listening for the sound of the front door, convincing myself I'll hear it open. That he'll come back, that maybe I'll wake up and last night won't feel so final.

But morning comes anyway.

I shower without thinking, pull on clothes I don't remember choosing. I stare at the stove long enough to wonder how many times he's made breakfast here. For me. Without me asking.

And then I leave.

I drive across town in silence—no music, no distractions. Just the sound of my tires on the road and my heartbeat trying to break through my ribs.

Wes and Savannah live in a cottage-style house tucked between two streets that both have "Maple" in the name, which has always felt unnecessarily confusing, but somehow on brand for them.

I don't text, I don't call. I just show up.

Savannah answers the door barefoot, a coffee mug in hand, her eyes widening the second she sees me.

"Come in," she says, already stepping aside. "We were just talking about you."

That makes my stomach lurch.

"I'm not staying long," I say, even as I step inside.

"Sure," she says softly. "But there's muffins. And coffee."

Wes leans around the corner, expression unreadable. "You okay?"

I open my mouth to lie.

And fail.

Savannah sets the mug down in front of me, then pauses a second too long, her eyes sweeping over my face. Not judgmental—just quietly observant. Like she's trying to fill in the blanks with the pieces I'm not saying out loud.

Wes, meanwhile, is still focused on his coffee like it's a tactical decision.

"You wanna talk about it?" Savannah asks, gentle.

I shrug. "He left."

Her gaze flicks briefly to Wes, who doesn't even flinch.

"Wait, who left?" he asks, not following.

"Gabe," I say. "After a fight. Last night."

Wes frowns, confused. "Why were you guys even fighting?"

Savannah doesn't say anything, but her brow arches just slightly. She knows we've hooked up in the past, she even knows I've had feelings for him, but I've always downplayed it. I'm sure she knows more than she lets on, or at least suspects.

Wes, though? Wes still thinks I'm the same girl who got heart-eyes for Gabe Keaton back when we were all too young to know better—only a couple years ago, though it feels like a lifetime. The same girl who used to swear she was so over it, even when it was obvious she wasn't.

I glance at Savannah, and the softness in her eyes damn near guts me. She's not surprised. She's sad for me.

Wes, bless him, just rubs a hand down his face and says, "Okay, clearly I'm missing something."

"You're not," I lie. "Not really."

Savannah gives me a look but doesn't push. Instead, she picks up the leash hanging by the back door. "I'm gonna take Daisy out," she says casually, like it's not a complete favor. Like she's not giving me space on purpose. "Text me if you need anything."

I nod, and she's gone from the room, barreling toward the tiny dog perched on the end of the stairs. She whistles to get the attention of their brand-new goldendoodle puppy Wes insisted on them getting settled before the baby comes. Something about "every kid needs to grow up with a dog."

Wes watches the door close behind Savannah, then turns to face me fully. Arms crossed, brow furrowed. "All right. What the hell's going on?"

I open my mouth, but nothing comes out. My stomach knots.

"You and Gabe." His voice is careful now. "It's more than it was, right?"

I blink. "What do you think it was?"

He shrugs. "You had a thing for him. Back in the day. I figured it fizzled out or turned into the weird friendship thing you two do."

I let out a dry laugh. "It was never just a friendship."

Wes raises a brow. "So what is it now?"

I shake my head. "I don't know."

But that's a lie. I *do* know; I just don't want to say it out loud, because then it's real.

Wes lets the silence stretch before he says, "Savannah said he's been different since moving in. I didn't think much of it, thought maybe he was just mellowing out now that he stopped getting back with Kara."

"He's been different," I admit. "But so have I."

Wes stares at me for a second, then leans on the counter. "Is that a good thing?"

I hesitate. "Yeah. It was."

"What happened?"

"I told him to leave."

His eyebrows shoot up.

"I didn't mean it," I rush to add. "It was in the middle of a fight. I was spiraling. But he left. And now I don't know if he's coming back."

Wes is quiet for a second, then says, "You love him?"

I let out a breath. "Yeah."

"Okay," he says simply, like it's not the biggest thing in the world. "Then fix it."

"It's not that simple."

"Why not?"

"Because I said things I can't take back. Because I made him feel like he was just...a mistake I kept making. And because—" I pause, pressing the heel of my palm to my chest. "Because I'm scared."

"Of what?"

"That if I ask him to stay, he won't."

Wes doesn't say anything for a moment. Then, softly, "Maybe he just needs a reason to."

I nod slowly, swallowing around the lump in my throat.

"And," he says, nudging my elbow, "I'm guessing this fight wasn't just about him."

I manage a weak smile. "No. Harry's selling the bar."

His brow furrows again. "Since when?"

"He has the paperwork. He doesn't seem particularly excited about it, but he's not backing out."

Wes exhales. "Damn."

"Yeah."

I tuck my legs up onto the bottom bar of the stool next to me, cradling the coffee Savannah made like it might steady me. "He told me I should buy it."

Wes blinks. "What?"

"The bar. Gabe said I should buy it." I laugh, but it comes out thin and uneven. "Like it's that simple. Like I could just slap my name on the deed and suddenly I'm qualified to run a business."

Wes doesn't laugh. He just tilts his head. "Okay...but why is that crazy?"

I stare at him. "Seriously?"

He shrugs. "You've been managing half the place for a while now without the title. You know the staff, the regulars, the vendors. You practically run the calendar and the inventory. If anyone knows how that bar works, it's you."

"But I've never owned anything like that. I don't know how to do taxes or...hire an accountant or whatever."

"Neither did Harry when he started. He figured it out."

"Yeah, well, Harry's not me."

Wes gives me a look. "No, he's not. You're better with people. You give a shit when someone's having a bad day. You catch things he misses."

I shake my head. "Wes..."

"I'm not saying it wouldn't be hard. I'm saying it's not insane. Not even a little."

I look down at my coffee. My hands are trembling just a little.

"I thought you'd say it was a terrible idea," I admit.

Wes goes still. "Why would you think that?"

"Because..." I pause, struggling to find the words. "Because I've never stuck with anything. Because every time I do, it feels like I disappoint someone. Usually you."

His brow furrows sharply. "Sage—"

"I know you didn't mean to," I cut in gently. "But when you'd get that look—like you were waiting for me to crash and burn, or when you'd offer to cover rent and then follow it with advice I never asked for...it always felt like you were waiting for me to grow up. Like I wasn't enough the way I was."

He leans back, jaw tight. But not defensive. Just...hurt. On my behalf.

"I thought I was helping," he says finally. "Trying to keep you safe. I thought you'd get sick of bouncing around and one day want something solid. I didn't realize I was part of the reason you never let yourself believe you already had it in you."

His voice is low, raw with guilt.

"I'm sorry," he adds. "I should've told you a long time ago that I was proud of you."

That undoes me a little. I look away, blinking fast.

Wes nudges my foot with his. "You're not a screw-up, Sage. You've always been the brave one. You just haven't had anyone back you when it really counted. So if this is what you want—the bar, the risk—I'll back you. All the way."

My throat closes around a lump. "But what if I fail?" I whisper. "What if I screw it up, and that's it—that's Mom's legacy down the drain?"

His expression shifts again, softer this time. Tired in the way grief never fully stops being.

"We both know where the money would come from," I add, voice barely above a breath. "I've never touched it. Not for anything. Not even when I really could've used it. Because I didn't want to waste it on something that wouldn't last."

Wes exhales, steady and long. He's quiet for a moment before he says, "That money isn't her legacy."

I blink at him.

"You are."

My heart stutters.

"She didn't leave it behind so you could be afraid of it," he says. "She left it because she wanted you to have something to build on. To believe in yourself when everything else felt uncertain."

I shake my head, though I'm not disagreeing—I'm just trying to keep from crying. Again.

"She'd want you to try," Wes finishes gently. "And honestly? So do I."

I press the heel of my palm to my eye and nod, once, sharply. "Okay."

"You sure?"

"No," I admit with a wobbly breath. "But I think I want to be."

He gives a small smile. "Good enough for me." Wes leans back again, quieter now. "You know you don't have to figure it out alone, right? You could talk to Jamie."

I blink. "Jamie?"

"Our advisor," he says, like it's obvious. "We've both had the same one since the trusts were set up. You don't have to commit to anything. Just...see what your options are."

I shift uncomfortably. "I don't even know if the trust is meant for something like this."

"It's meant for your future," he says, firm but not harsh. "And if this is what you want, really want, then that's exactly what it's for."

I pick at a loose thread on the hem of my sweatshirt. "I always thought using it meant wasting it."

"It put me through med school," he reminds me. "Nearly debt-free. Do you know how rare that is?" He shakes his head a little. "Mom didn't leave that money for us to hoard it out of fear. She left it so we could build something real with it."

The words hit me somewhere deep. It's something I didn't even know I needed to hear.

"She believed in us, Sage. You don't have to be her to prove you're worthy of it."

I nod, but it catches in my throat. "I don't even remember her," I admit, my voice coming out smaller than I mean for it to. "Not really. Just flashes, her perfume. The sound of her heels on the tile, the way she used to hum while she braided my hair."

Wes's expression softens, grief flickering behind his eyes in a way I don't often see from him.

"I was so young," I continue, voice wobbling. "And then she was just...gone. Everyone always talks about how smart she was. How successful, how fearless, but to me, she's more of a myth than a person. I don't remember what it felt like to be loved by her. Not really."

Wes exhales slowly. "You were loved, Sage. I promise you that."

I nod again, biting the inside of my cheek. "I just don't want to screw this up and feel like I wasted what little I have left of her."

"You wouldn't be wasting it," he says gently. "You'd be honoring it. You'd be doing what she always did—taking a risk, betting on yourself. You might not remember her clearly, but you've got more of her in you than you think."

I blink hard, fighting the sting behind my eyes.

"Call Jamie," he says again, voice softer now. "See what's possible. You don't have to decide anything today."

I nod one last time, this time steady. "Okay. I will."

Wes watches me for a second longer, then adds quietly, "And call Gabe."

I look up at him, startled.

He shrugs, like it's obvious. "You don't have to fix everything today, but that doesn't mean you should let it stay broken."

My throat tightens again. "What if he doesn't pick up?"

"Then try again tomorrow," he says. "And the next day. Until he knows you mean it."

I stare at him, unsure of what to say.

Wes rises from his chair with a soft groan and mutters, "Fine. If you won't call him, I'll call him myself. Be the overprotective big brother I probably should've been years ago."

I let out a surprised laugh, wet and shaky. "You wouldn't."

He lifts a brow. "You know I've got his number; we're friends, after all. I'll threaten him with a PowerPoint presentation on why he's an idiot if he walks away from you."

That gets a real smile out of me—small, but real. "You're a menace."

He shrugs. "Menace or not, I'm here. Always have been, even if I didn't always show it the right way."

I stand and wrap my arms around him before I can talk myself out of it. "You're a great brother, Wes."

He squeezes me back, tighter than I expect. "Took me long enough to earn that, but...thanks."

Neither of us says anything else for a moment. But I think he knows. I think we both do.

SIXTEEN

GABE

I hadn't planned on coming back.

Not after the way she looked at me when she told me to leave. Like I'd already let her down, like she was bracing for it, like part of her had been waiting for this ending the whole time.

But I couldn't stay away.

Not because I thought she'd change her mind—but because my toothbrush was still in the cup by the sink and my hoodie was draped over the living room chair. All my belongings were still here and I hadn't figured out how to live in a world where none of that meant anything anymore.

So I came back. Quietly, key barely turning in the lock, breath held in my chest, like if I made a sound it might shatter what little remained.

I told myself I'd just grab my stuff and be gone before she got home. Leave a note—pathetic, but better than nothing. Something honest, for once. Something she could read without me hovering, without me hoping.

But then the door opens.

And everything in me stills.

She steps into the apartment like she always has, but I can tell—she knows I'm here. Her energy changes, stretches taut across the silence like a held breath.

Before I know it, she's standing in my bedroom doorway.

Then: "You came back."

I stay facing the duffel bag. I don't trust myself to look at her, not yet. "Just to grab my stuff."

It's not bitter, it's not a jab. It's the closest I can get to the truth without bleeding out on the floor.

A pause.

Then: "You weren't even going to say goodbye?"

Her voice is quieter than I expect. Not angry. Just tired. Wounded in that way she never lets anyone see.

I swallow hard. "Didn't think I had a reason to."

It sounds crueler than I mean it to. What I meant was: I didn't think she'd want me to.

"You left a letter."

I glance at her hand, and sure enough, the envelope's there, creased in the middle, a smudge of flour or maybe dust still lingering on the edge. I don't know why I notice that—maybe because I'd set it down thinking it would sit there unread. Or maybe because the way she holds it, tight, careful, like it matters, makes it feel heavier than I'd meant it to be.

"I thought..." My voice is rough, and I clear it. "I thought it would be easier."

She doesn't say anything right away, just opens the flap.

And then, slowly, she begins to read.

Sage,

I know a letter is the coward's way out. But I've been a coward for a long time when it comes to you, so I figured I might as well finish the job in character.

I don't know where to start, because everything feels like it comes out wrong when it's about you. So maybe I just say this: I'm sorry.

I'm sorry for all the times I made you feel like you were temporary. Like you were something I could reach for only when the world fell apart. The truth is, you were the only thing that ever made sense, and that scared the hell out of me. So I kept pushing you away. I told myself you'd leave eventually anyway, because that was easier than admitting I was the one who didn't deserve to stay.

I'm sorry for Kara. For the way I let her hang around long after she should've been gone. I wasn't in love with her anymore, Sage, not in the way that counts. But she reminded me of my mom in a lot of ways. The chaos, the volatility, the way love was always tied to control and crisis. It felt familiar. Broken, but safe in its own warped way. She knew how to need me in a way that didn't ask for too much. With her, I could keep hiding.

With you, it was always different.

You never needed me. You just wanted me. And I didn't know how to sit with that. Didn't know how to be chosen without it feeling like a trap. You didn't ask me to save you. You just asked me to show up, and I didn't know how.

I don't blame you for what you said. You were right. I was a mess, and I used you as a soft place to land. But I wasn't using you to forget someone else. I was using you to remember what it felt like to hope for more.

I've changed, but that doesn't undo the way I hurt you. I'm not asking for a clean slate. I just needed you to know the truth.

You asked me why I kept pushing you about the bar. It's not because I think it's easy or because I thought you owed it to Harry, it's because I've seen you come alive behind that counter. Because I believe in you, even when you don't.

You're not a placeholder, Sage. You never were. You're the whole damn story. You're the chapter I wasn't brave enough to write until now.

I love you. I think I've loved you since the first time you made fun of me for drinking IPAs.

If you never want to speak to me again, I'll understand. But if some part of you still believes in second chances, I'll be here.

Even if it's just to cheer you on from the crowd when you make it on your own.

Always yours,
Gabe.

Her eyes stay on the page long after the words have stopped.

I watch her chest rise and fall, slow and shallow, like she's trying not to breathe too hard, like even that might break her open. Her fingers tremble just slightly at the edges, but she doesn't drop the letter.

When she finally looks up at me, her eyes are misty, glassy with something too big to name. Not quite tears, not yet, but close.

She swallows, mouth parting like she wants to say something, but no sound comes out. Her gaze flicks back down, like maybe if she reads it again, she'll understand how real it is.

I take a step forward before I even realize it, instinct more than choice. But I stop myself, give her space, even though everything in me wants to close the distance.

"I meant every word," I say softly. "Even the ones that make me sound like an idiot."

Her lips twitch. Barely, but it's there.

"I've never had anyone say they love me before," she says quietly. "Not in a romantic way, anyway."

My heart cracks a little, then a lot. "You should've heard it a long time ago."

She blinks hard, once, twice, like she's trying to blink it all away. But it clings to her anyway—the letter, the truth, the weight of everything unsaid finally let loose.

Then: "I just got off the phone with Harry."

I still. Her voice is steadier now, but not guarded. Open. Like she's walking toward something instead of running away.

"I called Jamie, Wes and I's financial advisor for the trust. I asked her what it would take—I'm gonna do it, Gabe. I'm going to buy the bar."

The air shifts.

Just like that, I know I'm looking at the bravest girl I've ever known—standing there, braids pulled back in a hasty bun, fingers curled around my cowardly letter like it's sacred, like it mattered.

"You're serious?" I breathe.

She nods. "Terrified. But yeah."

I take a breath like I haven't since she told me to leave. "Sage—"

She crosses the room before I can finish, and suddenly, she's in front of me. Her hands find my shirt, balling in the fabric. I don't hesitate. I reach for her, and this time, she lets me.

She melts into me like a home I forgot how to find.

I hold her tighter, not because I'm afraid she'll slip away again, but because I finally believe she won't. That we're not just circling each other anymore—we've landed.

Her voice is muffled against my chest when she says, "Don't leave again."

"I won't," I whisper, pressing my lips to the top of her head. "Not unless you tell me to. And even then...I'll probably wait on the porch."

She lets out a shaky laugh, the sound wet and real and beautiful. "We don't have a porch."

"Then I'll wait by the door."

We stay like that for a long time. No grand declarations, no promises we can't keep, just two people who finally stopped running—quiet, steady, and holding on.

And this time, neither of us lets go.

EPILOGUE
GABE

The thing about Harry's is—it still smells the same.

Beer-soaked wood and fryer oil, cheap whiskey and too-loud laughter. But the lighting's better. The bathrooms are cleaner. There's a framed photo of Sage and Harry behind the bar now, taken on her first official day as the new owner. She's grinning, arms thrown around his shoulders like the future never scared her at all.

I still remember the way her hands shook when she signed the paperwork. How she pressed her forehead to mine that night and whispered, "I don't know if I can do this."

And how I whispered back, "You already are."

Today, the place is packed for lunch, which is not so unusual anymore. Office regulars, neighborhood weirdos, a couple hungover college kids ordering greasy fries like they're sacred.

If I'm honest, I'm just glad to have somewhere with decent food now that isn't that fucking roast chicken from Andre's Liam doesn't shut up about.

Sage moves through the customers like she's been doing this her whole life. Her microbraids are twisted into a haphazard bun, a loose tee with the bar's new logo scrawled across the chest, laughter riding easy on her lips.

She doesn't notice me yet, so I let myself watch her a little longer.

Behind her, at one of the pub tables, Wes and Savannah are halfway through a basket of nachos. Savannah's got their new baby cradled in one arm, effortlessly bouncing her knee while gesturing with a chicken wing in the other.

Savannah catches me looking and shoots me a knowing grin over her wing. Wes follows her gaze, then lifts his drink in salute, like I'm not already here three times a week.

I head toward the bar, dodging a guy trying to order shots at noon and slipping into the space Sage just vacated. She turns a second later and startles when she sees me.

"Jesus, Keaton. Lurk harder."

I shrug. "Didn't want to throw off your groove."

"*My groove*," she repeats flatly, but she's fighting a smile.

We watched my favorite movie from when I was a kid last night, now I can't stop quoting *The Emperor's New Groove*.

She pulls two clean glasses from the rack and pours us each a soda without asking. No ice, extra lime in mine. It's a stupid thing, but it still makes my chest feel too full.

We lean against the bar, not talking for a moment. Just watching. A playlist she made months ago hums through the speakers, and someone yells "Fuck!" from the pool table corner, followed by a very apologetic "Sorry! Baby!"

Savannah doesn't flinch. Loretta Joy is snoring in her wrap like she's heard worse in the womb.

"She's got your lungs," I say, nodding toward the bundle in Savannah's arms.

Sage huffs a laugh. "She's got our mom's name."

"She'd be proud," I say, and I mean it.

Sage looks away for a beat, like she needs to blink something back, then clears her throat and lifts her chin. "She would." She tugs the towel off her shoulder and flicks it at my hip, as though trying to shake off the softness of the moment.

I let her pretend.

A few seats down, one of the regulars hollers something about the jukebox being "possessed again," and Sage rolls her eyes. "It's not possessed, it's just temperamental," she mutters, already stepping out from behind the bar to deal with it.

When she returns, wiping her hands on the towel, she finds me exactly where she left me. Still watching her.

"What?" she asks, cocking a brow.

"You broke the rules."

Her nose scrunches like she's already regretting coming back. "Don't start."

This has turned into somewhat of a bit between us, usually when the other one seems to grow irritated to get them to crack a smile.

I lean in on my elbows, grin tugging at my mouth. "No sex with roommates—that was the rule."

She scoffs. "You're lucky I don't put that on a sign behind the bar."

"You'd have to list all the rules you broke, though," I point out. "Might not fit on one sign."

She narrows her eyes. "You're awfully smug for someone who showed up with a duffel bag and a half-baked excuse about needing a place to crash."

I smirk. "It wasn't half-baked. Wes said I could stay."

"Wes didn't know you were in love with me."

"Details," I say, lifting my glass.

"Pretty big one, don't you think?"

"Didn't hear you complaining when I made you coffee every morning."

"That was bribery."

"Worked, didn't it?"

I tilt my head, pretending to think. "It was all worth it."

"You're ridiculous."

"You're the one who broke the rules."

"Tonight, maybe?" I ask, voice low.

Her brow arches. "What, break the rules again?"

I grin, but there's a flicker of something else behind it—something softer. "Sleep with your roommate."

She snorts. "We share a room now, dumbass."

Right, we do. The spare room's just a glorified guest room these days—though Wes once joked he'd rather burn it down than subject another poor, unsuspecting soul to living with us. Said it with a shake of his head and a smile that almost looked fond.

I glance down at her, this girl who used to flinch when I got too close and now steals the covers at night. And I think about how none of this was ever the plan—not for me, not for her—but somehow, it feels exactly like where we were supposed to end up.

"Still counts," I murmur. "Technically."

The charged silence that falls between us isn't heavy. It's full—of everything we've built, of everything we risked, of everything we chose.

She leans against the bar again, close enough that our arms brush.

From behind us, Loretta lets out a high-pitched squeal, and Savannah coos, "Tell Uncle Gabe to stop flirting and come hold you, huh?"

Sage's head tilts, amused. "Uncle Gabe, huh?"

"I'm part of the family now," I say, bumping her shoulder. "Better get used to it."

She hums like she's considering it, but her smile is already giving her away.

And honestly?

I hope I never stop earning it.

EXTENDED EPILOGUE

GROUP CHAT NAME: UNOFFICIAL EMERGENCY CONTACT LIST

SAVANNAH

loretta just sprinted through the kitchen yelling
NOOOOOO at the dog so. that's where we're
at now.

WES

she's fine. she's developing leadership skills.

SAGE

your toddler just told a 70lb goldendoodle "no"
like she pays the rent.

SAVANNAH

future president. or cult leader. TBD.

HANNAH

at this point in history, definitely the same thing.

JACKSON

morning chaos energy is strong today.

GEN

speak for yourself, i slept in. baby says I'm
allowed.

SAVANNAH

👀

WES

…gen.

SAGE

WAIT.

GABE

you're pregnant?!

SAVANNAH

shit.

GEN

saaaaav 😅

SAVANNAH

how is this my fault? you said it, i just reacted!

HANNAH

EXCUSE ME?! i have to learn about this with the peasants??

GEN

you already knew!!

HANNAH

NOT THE POINT.

LIAM

she literally texted us a sonogram last week.

HANNAH

still. principle.

SAGE

oh my god 🥺

GABE

we're gonna need a bigger brunch table.

JACKSON

due december. we're waiting to find out the gender.

SAVANNAH

i love how you say we're waiting like it wasn't your idea.

WES

calling it now, another girl. just to keep jackson on his toes.

GABE

loretta can show her how to rule with fear.

SAGE

we're starting a matriarchy.

HANNAH

as we should.

GEN

thank you for the chaotic congratulations. truly feeling the love.

SAGE

speaking of love... gabe and i put in the offer on that townhouse. we close next week.

SAVANNAH

I KNEW IT.

HANNAH

OMG congrats! city-adjacent soft life!

LIAM

do I still get a couch to crash on or

HANNAH

shut up liam.

GABE

only if you're on dog-sitting duty.

LIAM

betrayed.

JACKSON

everyone's thriving and I'm just over here
googling how much babies eat.

WES

24/7. they eat 24/7.

GEN

don't scare him.

SAVANNAH

too late.

SAGE

i love you all so much.

HANNAH

gross.

WES

someone end the thread before we start doing
group affirmations.

SAGE

i'm making a canva graphic right now.

GABE

please don't.

LIAM

too late. you know she has the app.

HANNAH

also, if anyone's wondering why I ghosted for a
week, it's because I'm bouncing between atlanta
and new york again. evita waits for no one.

SAGE

you used to sing don't cry for me argentina in the
shower and now it's paying the bills. full circle.

LIAM

remember when you said you'd never live in new york again?

HANNAH

that was before I was famous.

READ MORE FROM NICOLE RYAN

Just Peachy

Second Chance Vacation (Just Peachy Book 1)
Gen & Jackson's story
Available now!

Mostly Loathing You (Just Peachy Book 2)
Hannah & Liam's story
Available now!

Standalones

The Very First Night
Kat & Tanner's story
Available now!

Under The Yule Moon
Fleur & Winnie's story
Coming November 2025

ABOUT THE AUTHOR

Hey, I'm Nicole Ryan. I write romance with heart, heat, and just enough emotional wreckage to keep things interesting. My books are for anyone who loves messy characters, slow burns, and maybe shedding a few tears when they least expect it.

I've been writing since I was a kid, mostly as an escape, and the one bright spot back then was hanging out with my grandma at the local paper where she worked as a copy editor. She believed in my stories before I did.

I'm a Libra, but let's be honest, my Virgo moon is the one running the show. I spend an alarming amount of time convincing myself I need just one more book, blaming my moods on the moon or retrograde, and pulling tarot cards I probably wasn't ready for.

facebook.com/nicoleryanbooks

instagram.com/nicoleryanbooks

tiktok.com/@nicoleryanbooks

ACKNOWLEDGMENTS

This story almost didn't exist.

I shelved it, convinced I didn't have the emotional bandwidth to write contemporary romance in a world that feels like it's burning. I wanted magic, escape, fantasy. Reentering the messy, grounded world of Just Peachy felt impossible. And honestly? Painful. Gabe and Sage's story has always lived closest to my heart, and that kind of proximity made it harder to write, not easier.

But something changed when I stepped away to write in another genre. I kept opening this file. Not with pressure. Not with a plan. Just curiosity. And slowly, through a different lens, the words returned. The banter, the hurt, the longing—so much of it came back clearer than before.

To my readers who kept asking, gently, if their story might ever be told: thank you. You reminded me it was worth revisiting. And to Arianna, who has believed in this book and in me from the very beginning: your encouragement means more than I can ever express. I'm lucky to have you as a reader, and even luckier to call you my friend.

Also, because I know you'll bring it up the second you read this: yes, if *Just Peachy* ever gets picked up for screen, you'd better at least get an audition to play Sage if only because you never shut up about her.

This past year has been one of the hardest I've ever had. I made the choice to step back, to take care of myself, and to let go of people and patterns that no longer aligned with the version of me

I'm trying to become. And I know you noticed. I went from releasing three books in a year to... none. I crashed. Hard.

But I didn't disappear.

I spent that time honing my craft. Taking workshops, studying the kind of writing that stirs something in you, pushing myself to go deeper, and trying to make every word count. I worked on my voice, my prose, my purpose. And I hope it shows.

Sage and Gabe's story ended up coming out in a way I never expected, much more concise than originally planned. It was the shift I didn't know I needed. I ultimately decided to frame *Just Peachy* as a duet, centering the series around the two core siblings who launched the universe. And I stand by that. *One Room Vacancy* relies more heavily on the emotional threads of the first two books than any of the others, which is why I consider it a companion rather than a continuation. Still, it's special all on its own. And I hope it feels that way to you too.

To my incredible PA, Angel, thank you for being the only person who read this before my editor did, for cheering me on, and for never letting me forget that this story mattered. And to my amazing editor, Erin, thank you for your thoughtful eye, your steady support, and your trust in my voice.

To my readers, you, thank you. For sticking around. For waiting. For believing in these stories even when I wasn't sure I still could. Your support, your messages, your love... it's the reason I kept coming back to this manuscript. You helped me find my way again. I hope this story makes you feel seen. I hope it reminds you that second chances are real, even when they're messy. Especially when they're messy.

Thank you for letting me share Sage and Gabe with you. They've waited a long time. So have I.

www.ingramcontent.com/pod-product-compliance
Lightning Source LLC
Chambersburg PA
CBHW060456300726
48975CB00008B/2534